The Heritage of Literature Series

WITCH AND OTHER STORIES

The Heritage of Literature Series

Founder General Editor: E.W. Parker, M.C.

The titles in this series include modern classics, and a range of prose, poetry, and drama

A selection from the series includes

A complete list of the series is available on request

WITCH AND OTHER STORIES

with an introduction

GEORGE MACKAY BROWN

with commentary and notes by
D.M. BUDGE

LONGMAN

Longman Group Limited
London
Associated companies, branches and
representatives throughout the world

Text of *Witch and Other Stories*
© George Mackay Brown, 1967, 1969, and 1974
from the volumes, *A Calendar of Love*, *A Time to Keep*,
and *Hawkfall*.
Heritage of Literature Series commentary and notes
© Longman Group Ltd 1977

This edition first published by Longman Group Ltd
in association with The Hogarth Press 1977

ISBN 0 582 34916 8

Printed in Hong Kong by
Wing King Tong Co Ltd

CONTENTS

INTRODUCTION

Orkney, which is the setting of all the stories in this book, is a group of islands off the north coast of Scotland. About 17,000 people live there, of mixed Norse and Celtic and Scottish descent. The main industries are farming and fishing; but these are soon to be rivalled by the extensive operations resulting from the discovery of oil in the North Sea. (No one can say yet how oil will affect the islanders' way of life.) The islands are mostly fertile and well farmed. The capital is Kirkwall, a city by virtue of its Cathedral of Saint Magnus, which dates from the twelfth century. There is another smaller town on the west side of the main island – Stromness (which I call Hamnavoe in my stories and poems). There are several scattered villages. The islands for the most part rise gently from the sea; they have been likened to 'sleeping whales'. But there is one mountainous island, Hoy, which seems more Highland than Orcadian. To the west is the Atlantic Ocean: Orkney meets its rages with a long battlement of superb cliffs. To the east is the North Sea, with its fish and oil. North-east of Orkney are the Shetland Islands, and beyond them to the north-west, the Faeroes and Iceland. The seas between were the familiar 'swan's way' and 'whale's acre' to the most famous Orkneymen in history, the Vikings.

I was fortunate to be born in a community where the art of story-telling had been practised for many generations. All islands from the beginning of time are natural breeding-grounds for story and legend. The people in islands are a close-woven community; they are naturally interested in each other, and in the families that intermarry and trade and quarrel, and flourish and fade. The sea is all around, that mysterious dangerous fruitful element. Strange objects come in on the tide: spars, a salted boot, a box of apples. Hardly a winter passed in the old days that a ship was not wrecked on this island or that; in those lean times it was a godsend for a poor community; down the huge crags men swarmed to plunder the holds.

Hardly a winter passed, too, without a local fishing boat being lost in the dark storms that sweep suddenly over the North Atlantic.

So, islanders have had always this ambivalent attitude to the sea. It gave them fish and wrecked cargoes, it brought foreign gold to the tills of merchant and ale-house keepers, it satisfied the young men's perennial hunger for adventure. And yet there is a constant image throughout the history of any island: the women waiting at the shore at dawn and sunset, with fate on their faces, either for the boats to come home laden with the living silver of the sea, or for the bodies of their menfolk to be washed ashore after a storm.

Islands too are generally places of large and small farms. There is something peculiarly quickening to the imagination of a storyteller in this interweaving of sea and land, tilth and salt. Work on the land is slow and sure: it has a definite pattern throughout the year: it is a ritual of fruitfulness. Of course there are years of drought and hunger from time to time, but in general the safe rhythms of the soil are utterly different from the savage incalculable sea rhythms.

In former centuries, islanders were so poor that the earth-workers had to build themselves boats for fishing. It is in contrast that a storyteller finds his greatest delight, and there can be no greater contrast than the primitive elements of land and sea out of which men have, with danger and endurance, to drag their livelihood.

Winters in the north are long and dark and cold. It is round hearthflames that the first stories were told: an old wise remembering mouth, a circle of entranced listeners. What they hear are tales of their great-grandfathers (for present

events are still gossip and speculation and not yet suitable to
be the vintage of narrative). Further back the stories go, long
beyond the remembrance of the storyteller at the fire; then
all unnecessary details are left out, such as the colour of a
character's eyes or the acreage of his fields, and out of the
starkness the hero looms larger than life, and every word he
utters is simple and portentous. Then the tale is more a legend
than a story.

Apart from the doings of their ancestors, these islanders
were fascinated by fate and chance and the mysteries they
observed all around them. Where did they come from? Where
were they going? What makes the sea salt? What keeps the
winter sun from cooling to a cinder? Is a man free or fated?
Why is one man born cripple and another a maker of music?
How can a beautiful girl fall in love with an old ugly poor
man, or with a seal? What promises and dooms are written
across the night? What makes the corn grow? What is the
bond between men and animals, dust and seed and sun?

These wonderings are perennial; without them storytellers
and poets would have vanished from the earth. The oldest
questions and the earliest attempts to explain in words the
burden of the mystery can, I suppose, be called myth. Gods
and dragons and trolls intermingle familiarly with men and
women. Nowadays we have other names for the great forces
that act up on nations and families and individuals, and keep the
stars in their courses; these forces are expressed in numbers,
diagrams, tables of statistics and graphs, rather than in words
and images. In a civilization dominated increasingly by
numbers, myths are museum pieces. It may be that the legend
and the story will wither too, in time, as the power of the
number grows. Meantime – thankfully for people like me –
ordinary folk still take delight in a story.

I am inclined to think that a really great story – like Tolstoy's
'What Men Live By', or Daudet's 'La Mule du Pape', or
Forster's 'The Road to Colonus' – have a mingling of myth

and legend in them. There are firstrate storytellers (I think of Maugham) into whose tales these elements do not enter; the tales remain, however superb the craftmanship, unsatisfying, as if some basic hunger in our nature is not being attended to.

The Orkney islands have been continually inhabited for six thousand years at least. We do not know what primitive magical myths entranced the Neolithic tribes in their stone villages beside the sea; nor what intricate patterned tales were told by the Pictish storytellers who succeeded them. But it is certain that some images and symbols remain like fossils embedded in our folklore.

When the Norsemen came out of the east and conquered the Picts the mists were suddenly dispelled. The great art of those sea rovers and settlers was narrative. They were superb storytellers. Their kinsmen in Iceland told some of the world's greatest stories in their sagas: *Burnt Njal*, *Laxdale*, etc. We have our own *Orkney Saga*, which tells the stories over centuries of the Norse earls of Orkney and their friends and enemies. It is an anthology of superbly told happenings: the feud between Earl Thorfinn and Earl Rognvald the First; the martyrdom of Saint Magnus; the Jerusalem pilgrimage in the twelfth century of Earl Rognvald the Second, a story tumultuous with heroes and villains, war and sanctity. After the Viking age, Scotsmen came increasingly to have power and influence in Orkney. The Scots are no mean storytellers either: their narrative ballads are among the greatest in the world. The realism of the Norse was leavened with Celtic mysticism and 'faery'. One of our finest stories, *The Play of The Lady Odivere*, exhibits the fruitful mingling to perfection. We can almost hear the harp-strokes and intonings of the bard beside the great hearth of the Stuart earls in Birsay or Kirkwall.

A long dark time settled in Orkney in the seventeenth and eighteenth centuries. The people were poor and oppressed. The great stories, like the sagas, were forgotten. We are back with the old remembering mouth and the flamelit listening faces round the hearth. Many of these stories – hundreds, perhaps – have been lost, for one reason and another. What remains – a mingling of magic and heroism and horror and cleverness and naivete – can be found in a fine recent book *The Folklore of Orkney and Shetland* by Ernest W. Marwick. I am not an isolated storyteller writing in the late twentieth century; I draw from a treasury of narrative written and unwritten out of the islands' past; many voices speak through me; I am part of a tradition.

People who have read translations of the Icelandic sagas will see how strongly they have influenced me in such stories as 'Jorkel Hayforks', 'Tartan', 'The Burning Harp'. I admire the 'pure' art of the sagamen; everything extraneous, such as detailed descriptions of people and places and comments by the author on what is happening, is ruthlessly excluded. Perhaps Hemingway of modern authors comes closest to that tough bare austere style.

But the mysterious dark centuries during which no stories were written down but many exciting things happened – I have been fascinated by that time also; there were the witches, the smugglers, the merchants, the great pirate Gow, the men of the pressgang. Undoubtedly the illiterate storyteller cele-brated these people, but the stories are lost, and so in a way I am trying, imaginatively, to fill up a gap in time with such stories as 'Witch', 'The Whaler's Return', 'Master Halcrow'.

I rarely write a story about the 1970s, for the reason given earlier in this introduction. Passing events are difficult to grasp, form, pattern. I feel more at home writing about the 1920s or the 1930s, when I was a small boy listening with wonderment, in the tailor's-shop where my father worked, to the old seamen and farmers weaving their verbal spells. Stories like 'A Time to Keep' and 'Tithonus' have something of the period flavour of my childhood.

A shadow lies over 'the story' today. I have spoken of how the number is taking over from the word. A symptom of this usurpation is the steady erosion of literary magazines in which writers can display their talents. There is great argument as to whether television will help or maim the publication of fiction. One thing is sure: a written story compels the reader to use his own imagination, he is an active participant with the author. No such fruitful cooperation occurs when you watch a story on television: a part of the creative faculty that exists in everybody is allowed to wither. Long then live the book; since the spoken story is heard nowadays only in lonely and unimportant places of the earth.

Such works as *The Odyssey*, *The Tempest* and *Twenty Years A-Growing* are steeped in the enchantment of islands. The imagination of men has dwelt long on such places as Atlantis and Tir-Nan-Og.

> Be not afeared, the isle is full of noises,
> Sounds and sweet airs that give delight and
> hurt not...

One mystery remains, which I cannot unravel. Most islands – the Hebrides, for example – are full of the 'sweet airs' that Shakespeare writes of; they have a rich tradition of song and music. This is not so in Orkney; music has never been the predominant art here, though each generation of Orkneymen has had its good fiddlers. Art in Orkney has devoted itself in the main to the production of stories: the noises and sounds come from the grave mouth of the storyteller.

GEORGE MACKAY BROWN

December 1975

COMMENTARY

George Mackay Brown is a poet, playwright, novelist and an acknowledged master of the short story. He has perfected a style which makes his writing instantly recognizable, and his best work has a fluent and magical quality. His achievements are formidable, yet his work consists almost entirely of a series of celebrations of past and present life in a little group of islands where he lives and was born.

The Orkney Islands are situated close to the tip of the north-east mainland of Scotland. Viewed on an atlas page the islands have a remote and unimportant appearance and they have long been a largely ignored part of the United Kingdom. The discovery in recent years of North Sea oil has restored the islands to a prominence which, apart from brief wartime spells of glory centred on the naval base at Scapa Flow, they have not known since the days of the Norse occupation.

Part of the great Scandinavian eruption that was eventually to reach as far as Arabia and the Black Sea, the land-hungry Viking marauders first arrived to plunder the Orkney Picts late in the eighth century. The islands presented land and a convenient base for further rampage and soon the Norsemen began to settle. A new way of life was imposed on Orkney and some of the Viking chiefs developed their own pattern of living, sowing their seed-corn in the spring, going west and south to plunder in the summer, and returning at harvest-time to prepare for a winter of ale and as much warmth as they could muster until the time for the planting of seeds came again. During the occupation the Picts as a people disappeared from the islands. Norse rule was absolute and a new language and culture took root in Orkney.

The coming of the Norsemen to Orkney had been proud

and violent: their going was quiet and expedient. An impoverished King Christian of Norway and Denmark, hard-pressed in 1468 to scrape together a dowry for his daughter Margaret, pledged the islands to James III of Scotland and the days of the Norse earls of Orkney were over. But the old ghosts of Scandinavia have never left Orkney. On islands already rich in the bones and artefacts of their early peoples the Norsemen left much to ensure that they would not easily be forgotten. In the placenames and in the Orkney Norn (the dialect of the islands) is locked their language, and in Kirkwall the Norse cathedral of St Magnus stands to this day. Yet the Norse place in the history of Orkney is secured not only by cultural and physical evidence of their occupation. When the Vikings first landed on the islands their chronicles were largely in the keeping of their storytellers and skalds (bards); when they left their deeds had been enshrined in the written words of the great Icelandic sagas.

The art of the saga evolved during the period of the Norse reign in Orkney, and sagatelling was one of the recognised accomplishments of a gentleman in medieval Iceland. Although probably all the Icelandic sagas had been committed to writing by the end of the twelfth century, the saga was essentially the province of the storyteller who leavened history with some historical fiction and directed his craft firmly towards the business of popular entertainment. His work had the blessing of a hopeful Icelandic Church anxious to provide the populace with alternatives to dancing and other morally dangerous pastimes.

The author of a saga adopted an austere and sometimes laconic approach to his work. His audience knew all about contemporary conventions of nobility, honour and formal hospitality. They knew about Icelandic law, and they believed in fate and the supernatural. Explanations of such matters the sagateller could, and did, ignore. As his stories were about people his listeners knew or at least had heard about, a concise

introductory genealogy was sufficient to remind his audience
of a family's characteristics. The author stated the name of
his hero, furnished a brief roll of his relatives, and then got
on with his tale. His aim was entertainment and his methods
were straightforward, impersonal and to the point. For writers
with some regard for the earlier tricks of their trade the saga
has much to offer in the way of a vigorous technique.

George Mackay Brown has not restored to the present day
the saga as a literary form, but he has taken its spirit, its tersely
economical style and concern for the small but illuminating
incident, and adapted it to his own ends. That he should
borrow from the past in his recreations of the past is no less
than fitting, although it is tempting to wonder what contribution
his years as Stromness correspondent of the now defunct
Orkney Herald have made to his economy of presentation.
Writers seeking to learn how to pare their prose seldom need
to look beyond the pertinent and skilful reporting to be found
in the columns of almost any local newspaper.

Behind, and occasionally in front of, the saga-like structure
of some of his stories there are strong biblical overtones and
a strange but acceptable ceremoniousness of speech. His
characters are resoundingly mortal and his stories explore a
world of struggling and sometimes quite unlovely humanity.
The element of struggle is often represented by obstacles more
spiritual than physical that have to be overcome before someone
can win through to find peace, or a prosaic and mundane
destiny, or sometimes both. Some, like Robert in 'The Wheel',
do not win through, but are confused and caught up in a
strange limbo. In 'The Whaler's Return' a man drives himself
through another kind of Pilgrim's Progress and, having at last
emerged from a maze of lures and pitfalls, is greeted not with
kiss or an embrace from his bride-to-be but with her flat
statement of the obvious: 'You're back from the whales,
Andrew Flaws.' As she acknowledges his return with a litany
of facts he prepares himself for a morrow which will set the

pattern of all his remaining days. The laird in 'Tithonus' survives to face a twilight of emptiness, while in 'Jorkell Hayforks' a man very near to the end of his days finally finds a way of making his peace. At the other end of the scale, the most joyous of George Mackay Brown's creations is 'The Seller of Silk Shirts'. The Sikh pedlar wheedles and flatters, shamelessly overcharges, and is happy. Perhaps because he is alien, and unmistakably an outsider, the writer felt free to allow him that exultation of the heart which he seldom and sparingly extends to his other characters.

The theme of 'Master Halcrow, Priest' is the ready betrayal of an old faith at the time of the Reformation, and the defiance of change is placed in the custody of an old priest who fishes too often and drinks too much. The story conveys a powerful sense of outrage and there is more than a hint of ferocity in the writing. Another betrayal provides the plot of the fine story 'Witch', where the writer's immaculate control of the emotional temper of language is seen at its best. The betrayal of human dignity and decency, and of justice and fair play, is presented calmly in a situation where many writers would have exploited in full the horrors and terrors of the victim's interrogation and fate. Unerringly, George Mackay Brown releases only one emotive phrase and writes of the mutilated prisoner hobbling to her execution 'with her fingers like a tangle of red roots at the end of her long white arms'. 'Witch' is a model exposition of one form of the short story.

It is his precise and caring use of language which sets George Mackay Brown apart, and there is a delicate restraint in his writing. Around a deceptive simplicity of style he fashions a shape and his best work has a perfect proportioning. The precision of his language imparts its own rhythm as each new word follows on with a satisfying inevitability. His careful use of words often gives rise to the concept of a procession, a moving ritual of language where each word has an ordered place in a ceremony of meaning.

His ceremonious use of language is particularly suited to his recreations of the past, and so overwhelming is a sense of the past in much of his work that George Mackay Brown is often thought of as a writer almost exclusively concerned with remote events. Yet of the forty-seven stories in his four published collections one is set in the future and the remainder evenly divided between the present century and the distant past. But it is worth noting that his solitary tale of the future depicts a world of villages, of small communities restricted to the most natural of resources; a world where poetry is supreme. It is as if from a belief that eternal truth is simple and uncomplicated the writer has created in 'The Seven Poets' (*The Sun's Net*, 1976) a world of the future where, in a reconstruction of an ideal past, the proper values of mankind are resurrected in a quasi-primeval society of sweetness and gentle simplicity. The story can be read as a postscript to his first novel *Greenvoe* (1972): the novel tells of the destruction of a community by the might of modern technology; the story spells out what one day may arise from technology's ashes. 'The Seven Poets' and 'The Tarn and the Rosary' are two stories rudimentary to any attempt at understanding George Mackay Brown's work and the potency of the forces behind it.

By his own account, George Mackay Brown lives and works in a community and in a place where all he needs as a writer is to hand. His sources are limitless and he is happiest, and his work at its best, when he reaches into the past. To his writing he properly brings his beliefs and his likes and dislikes. He is impatient with the bureaucracy of the modern state and the preponderance of 'isms'; he dislikes the overlordship of the machine and he is angry about the effect of Puritanism on people, society and religion. He is attached to the earth and the sea, to mysticism and old religions, pagan and Christian. A religious intensity burns in his work: religion, through ceremony, appears to be life itself to him, and it enables him to take a view of mankind that is sometimes breathtaking in its timelessness.

Religion in Orkney has been serenely Protestant since the Reformation. In four hundred years the only Catholic community of any size the islands have known was formed by the Italian prisoners of the Second World War who left behind their chapel on Lamb Holm as an enduring memorial of their time in Orkney. It is a measure of George Mackay Brown's commitment that, in his maturity, he proclaimed the strength of his beliefs by entering the Roman Catholic Church. The Catholic Church, guardian of an old faith, rich in ritual and ceremony, is perhaps a natural haven for a writer whose work displays an involvement with the ceremonial aspects of religion which is little less than passionate. As a writer versed in two opposing creeds he is advantageously in a position to exploit both, and he generally does so with great charity. But 'Master Halcrow, Priest', his tale based on the ejection by the Reformers of the priest from his church of St Peter's in Stromness in 1561, notably lacks charity, and the reader is left in no doubt of the author's view that at least one incident of the Reformation was a shabby and contemptible affair. The story brings out sharply the writer's rigorous attachment to those values which feature prominently in his stories, poems, plays and novels.

His attachments in many ways run counter to the mood of the times and his refusal to compromise and his stolid opposition to much that is contemporary lend an edge and a savour to his work. His strong dislike of Puritanism is no surprise when it is remembered that he has lived his life close to fishermen whose adherence to hellfire faiths is notorious. Nor does the voice of that arch-enemy of the Vatican, the Free Church of Scotland, go unheard in the islands of Orkney. There is a chill and a bleakness in extreme Protestantism and its tenets fall grievously on a poet's ear.

There is no one like George Mackay Brown writing in English today. He has written himself into a world recognizably his own. The clean, uncluttered and precise use of words is his hallmark and he weaves his themes like a tapestry, each story strengthening and lengthening the weave and adding further illumination.

A writer who goes so often to the same well, who returns again and again to similar themes, runs the considerable risk of writing himself out and becoming tiresome to his readers, and only immense craftsmanship can save the day. The sure application of his craft, as he deploys a rhythmic and sparing prose, is George Mackay Brown's saving grace. He is unmistakably his own man, a long way down a road of his own choosing, and his work demonstrates clearly that there is no need for him to turn back.

D.M. BUDGE

THE SELLER OF SILK SHIRTS

I crossed yesterday to the island of Quoylay to sell silk shirts to the people. I am a Sikh boy. My name over here is Johnny.

First was the boatman. He says to another man in the stern, in a voice that goes up and down like singing:

'Do what you like, says I,
But when in future
You want a loan of two pounds,
Don't come, says I, to my door,
Inga,
After what you said and did in the village on Saturday night.'

At the croft above the pier a man was building a new pig-sty. He was carrying stones from the beach. A boy was carrying stones from the beach. A girl also was carrying stones from the beach. The girl stopped and made tea . . . Those pigs have the expectation of living in a beautiful little house made of stones that have been under the sea.

There is a house where is a telephone and also a shop. Going to such a place I have made a mistake, they also sell shirts though coarse of cotton and wool, not silk shirts. This is strange, also they sell tobacco, sugar, rope, many things. The lady there was most fat and most kind.

I have gone then to a house on a hill. Many hens promenade at the door. I have much fear of the dog but there are words in the inside darkness that say, 'Down, Laddie, down.' What an old lady dusts the chair for my backside to sit! What an old man of words! His wrists were ornamented with blue anchors. Their ale was such that I might have fallen asleep on the chair. I have sold a silk scarf to the lady, that she will wear to the agricultural show next week, I am thinking.

Now did the next big house prove to be the minister's house. There are many unused rooms, none but the minister and his woman, what shame, a hundred of my people might live and sleep there. He has made remarks about bathing in the holy River Ganges that show signal knowledge. No refreshment, neither tea nor ale nor cigarettes, though I have complimented him on the immense number and blackness of his books.

Here is a beautiful girl living alone in a place with broken windows beside the loch. I make myself delightful to this girl. There is no dog. There is no old person behind the door angry. Instead there is a new round cake smoking on the table. This girl says, 'Lucky you have come today. At the week-end I had no money, my national assistance was spent. On Saturday night by hard means I got money in the village. Lucky you have come, I must buy a birthday present for Tom the boatman, a silk shirt would be beautiful.'

Yet she has not enough money for a silk shirt. Yet I have sold her one cheap, a bargain, a yellow silk shirt spread out wide like a sleeping butterfly on the little flowered bed she sleeps in.

Such was the beautiful poor girl I sold a shirt to, beside the loch. Her name was called Inga. Even so with the cheapness of the sale I had thirty-five per cent profit. Pretty was Inga.

Three things troubled me crossing the field to the hospitable farm of Greengyres. First, I entered inadvertently my foot into a rabbit hole. Second, I was threatened by a female cow with horns. Third, needing to pass water I was faced wherever I turned by near and distant windows. Yet at the delightful farm of Greengyres were met all my difficulties. There I sold no less than one shirt, four pairs sox, six handkerchiefs, all articles silken.

The schoolmistress was forbidding and in a mood to send me away till I have told her of my graduation from the Univer-

sity of Bombay with B.A. degree and the imminence of my
Ph.D. studying at the University of Edinburgh in October on
a thesis, 'The Topography of the Mystical Books of William
Blake'. She has graduated from that same university. She is
not like Inga, pretty. She has long black hairs on her lip, and
a wart.

Much walking I did on that island.

On the other side of the hill were three spreading peats,
a man and two women, in the sun. Here was much mirth.
I say to the man, 'You have no shirt, therefore you must buy
one of my silk shirts.' All laid down their implements with
laughter. A woman said, 'Nobody wears a silk shirt cutting
peats.' We laughed greatly. I then responded with this remark,
'Yet when the peats are cut and brought home, then will come
the hour of celebration that will necessitate the wearing of a
silk shirt!' There I stayed with merriment for five-and-twenty
minutes, drinking tea from a flask and smoking two cigarettes.
Truly these were merry peat-cutters.

In the evening at the stipulated hour I returned to the boat.
The boatman was saying to another man in the stern, but really
with the speech of those islanders it seems like singing:

> 'So then, what could I say?
> For my birthday
> Had she not baked a small cake
> And brought on her arm
> A shirt yellow as buttercups
>
> > this very afternoon?
>
> That way
> All our troubles ended.'

In the island of Quoylay I have sold seven shirts, three pairs
sox, twenty-one handkerchiefs, five scarves, and to Inga I
have given a free headsquare depicting the dance called 'The
Shake', though I have told her it was the god Krishna among
milkmaidens.

3

THE WHEEL

ON Saturday night in the fishermen's pub there's always plenty of noise and smoke. By nine o'clock you can hardly see the bottles at the far end of the bar for reek, and you have to shout to make yourself heard by the man at your elbow. There's darts and arguments and dominoes and stories going on all round, and the erratic jingling commerce of silver and glass across the bar.

At five past nine, as always, Robert appeared at the door. He said in his coarse throaty voice, 'Have any o' you men seen Walls?'

At once there was silence. The dart thrower held his hand. The drinkers paused in the act of lifting their pints. Old Tom the barman's hand froze on the lever. The whole pub was turned to stone for about one second.

'No,' said old Tom, 'he hasn't been here tonight.'

Robert turned and shambled out through the door.

Immediately the pub resumed its normal life. The dart flew at the board. The pints rose and fell. Money and glasses rang on the counter. The farmers sitting round the table laughed and pressed their knees. Everything went on as before, with perhaps a little more abandon, now that Robert had taken the gorgon's head away.

Robert followed the same ritual every Saturday night. His first visit was to the pub. His next call was to the Salvation Army ring at the pierhead.

The band and songsters were rendering 'Count your Blessings' when Robert arrived. He walked slowly over the cobbles and stood behind Miriam, a girl with big grey eyes and golden hair.

'Has Walls been here tonight?' he whispered to her.

4

Miriam, still singing, shook her head and smiled gently at Robert. One by one the girl Salvationists shook their heads at him. 'No,' whispered Miriam through the brazen clamour, 'not tonight. But some day soon we'll all be seeing him.'

Robert looked closely at the three men there, as if the face of Walls might be concealed under one of those black brims and blood-and-fire badges, behind one of those shining joyous instruments; for hadn't Walls once joined the Army in a fit of repentance after a drunken spree, and learned to play the cornet before he lapsed again...? But none of those faces belonged to the lost one. Robert turned away slowly.

He walked up the street to a narrow two-storey house. There the holy rag-time was no longer audible. He opened the outer door and climbed slowly upstairs. At the top of the house he tapped at a door with a printed notice on it: *H. Leask, Dressmaker.*

'Come in, Robert,' cried a deep voice from inside. Robert tip-toed in and sat down beside the fern.

A huge red-faced woman was seated at a sewing-machine, working on a dress for a young girl, half-finished, covered with alternate roses and swallows. All the time the woman spoke to Robert she went on working.

'What's new in the town tonight?' she said.

'There's nothing new at all,' said Robert, 'except that Harold the shepherd was disgraceful drunk in the pub, and the Army's given Miriam a new red band for her bonnet.'

'Fancy that,' said the woman.

There was a long difficult silence. Then Robert said, slowly and hesitatingly, 'I'm thinking o' turning owre the tattie patch in the morning...and I wanted to tell Walls...so he could order a load o' dung...but he hasna been home...and I was wondering...' His words trailed off into silence.

'You was wondering what?' said the woman patiently.

'I was wondering...the way he's always coming back and

5

fore here . . . maybe . . . if he was, you ken . . . up here beside you?'

She looked at Robert with her black eyes and said, 'No, Robert, I'm sorry to say he hasna been up here at all tonight, or any other night this while back.'

'O well, then I'll be going,' said Robert, getting to his feet.

She stopped work, listening to his clumsy feet going down the stair. She put her hand across her eyes and bent her head over the cloud of cotton, over the crumpled wings and crumpled petals. Her face was blank and streaming.

After that, Robert walked up the hill between the fields, to a stone house that looked out over the islands and the burning hills. He walked slowly now, as if he was afraid of something.

Even before he reached the door, as he stood lurching and hesitant on the gravel, it was opened by a neat little man with a beard and a grey polo-neck jersey. 'You'll be wanting to know about Walls,' said the man.

'Yes, captain,' said Robert timidly. 'Maybe you can tell me, for I mind him saying he might be coming to you for a reference, if he decides to go to the whaling next year.'

'I'll tell you,' said the man, 'the same as I've told you every Saturday night for the last two years.'

'No,' said Robert, 'don't tell me that.'

'I will tell you,' said the man, 'for it's the truth, and the sooner you realize it the better.'

'No,' said Robert, 'never mind, I'll go home.'

The old sailor seized him by the arm. 'Listen,' he said, in a loud angry voice. 'Walls is cold and in his grave. Didn't I see him laid out in the mortuary? Didn't I take the head of his coffin when we carried him to the kirkyard? Didn't I put a stone up for him, with his name and his years carved on it?'

Robert shook himself free. He gave the little man one terrified look. Then he turned between the new daffodils and the fuchsia bush on to the road. His feet shuffled and knocked into each other in his haste to be gone.

'You better behave yourself,' yelled the old sailor after him. 'You better not come annoying folk every Saturday night, asking after a dead man! There's places for fools like you! Now I'm warning you!'

At home in the little stone house at the edge of the pier, Robert laid the table for two, as he always did, and put on the kettle to boil. He opened a drawer in the dresser and thumbed through a pile of letters and cuttings. At last he found the scrap of newspaper he was looking for. He put on his steel spectacles, and sitting down in the straw-back chair beside the fire read the print on it:

'Last Saturday night a sad discovery was made, when the body of a local sailor William Walls was found at low tide among the rocks under his own pier. Mr Walls, who was fifty years of age, was of a jovial disposition, and will be much missed by his many friends in the locality. The news came as a particular shock to Mr Walls' cronies with whom he had spent a happy evening only a matter of hours before the tragic discovery was made. For some years he sailed in the Swallow Line under Captain Stevens, a distinguished son of the islands. Mr Walls was a bachelor, and lived at the South End with his friend Mr Robert Jansen, with whom sympathy is expressed at this time. The funeral, which was well attended, took place to the local cemetery on Tuesday afternoon, and was conducted by Lieutenant Rogers of the Salvation Army, with which sect the deceased had been connected at one period in his career.

Robert carefully replaced the cutting in the drawer. He put a spoon of sugar and a spurt of milk into each cup. He took two eggs out of the box and broke them into the pan; then, after a moment's hesitation, he broke a third egg into the pan.

'Walls is always hungry for his supper on a Saturday night, after the drink,' he murmured. 'What a man for eggs!'

7

WITCH

AND at the farm of Howe, she being in service there, we spoke directly to the woman Marian Isbister, and after laid bonds on her. She lay that night in the laird's house, in a narrow place under the roof.

In the morning, therefore, she not yet having broken fast, the laird comes to her.

LAIRD: Tell us thy name.

MARIAN: Thou knowest my name well. Was I not with thy lady at her confinement in winter?

LAIRD: Answer to the point, and with respect. Thy name.

MARIAN: I was called Marian Isbister in Christian baptism.

STEPHEN BUTTQUOY (who was likewise present and is a factor of the Earl of Orkney): And what name does thy dark master call thee?

LAIRD: What is thy age?

MARIAN: I was eighteen on Johnsmas Eve.

LAIRD: Art thou a witch?

At this, she raised her fists to her head and made no further answer.

That same day, in the afternoon, she was convoyed to Kirkwall on horseback, to the palace of the earl there. All that road she spoke not a word. There in Kirkwall a chain was hung between her arm and the stone.

Next morning came to her Andrew Monteith, chaplain to the earl.

MONTEITH: Thou needest not fear me. I am a man in holy orders.

MARIAN: I fear thee and everyone. My father should be here.

MONTEITH: Thou hast a scunner at me for that I am a man of God and thou art a servant of the devil.

MARIAN: How can I answer thee well? They keep food from me.

MONTEITH: I will speak for food to be given thee.

MARIAN: I thank thee then.

MONTEITH: Wilt thou not be plain with me?

MARIAN: All would say then, this was the cunning of the evil one, to make me speak plain. I do speak plain, for I am no witch, but a plain country girl.

MONTEITH: Thou art as miserable a wretch as ever sat against that wall.

MARIAN: I am indeed.

MONTEITH: Thy guilt is plain in thy face.

MARIAN: John St Clair should be here.

MONTEITH: What man is that?

MARIAN: The shepherd on Greenay Hill. He would not suffer thee to say such ill words against me.

MONTEITH: Is he thy sweetheart?

MARIAN: Often enough he called himself that.

That day, at noon, they gave her milk and fish and a barley cake, the which she ate properly, thanking God beforehand. They likewise provided her a vessel for the relief of nature. It was not thought well to give her a lamp at night.

So seven days passed, a total week. On the Sabbath she prayed much. She ate little that day, but prayed and wept.

On the Tuesday came to her cell William Bourtree, Simon Leslie, John Glaitness, and John Beaton, together with the chaplain, and two clerks (myself being one) to make due note of her utterances.

MONTEITH: Stand up, witch. Thou must suffer the witch's test on thy body.

MARIAN: I think shame to be seen naked before strange men. This will be a hard thing to endure. A woman should be near me.

They bring Janet, wife to William Bourtree.

JANET: I think none of you would have your wives and

daughters, no nor the beast in your field, dealt with thus.

She kissed Marian, and then unlaced her, she making now no objection.

Then the probe was put into the said Marian's body, in order to prove an area of insensitivity, the devil always honouring his servants in that style. These parts were probed: the breast, buttocks, shoulders, arms, thighs. Marian displayed signs of much suffering, as moaning, sweating, shivering, but uttered no words. On the seventh probe she lost her awareness and fell to the ground. They moved then to revive her with water.

JANET: She suffers much, at every stab of that thin knife, and yet I think she suffers more from your eyes and your hands – all that would be matter of laughter to a true witch.

Yet they still made three further trials of the probe at that session, Marian Isbister discovering much anguish of body at each insertion.

Then they leave her.

That night she slept little, nor did she eat and drink on the day following, and only a little water on the day following that. She asked much for Janet Bourtree, but Janet Bourtree was denied access to her.

On the eleventh day of her confinement a new face appeared to her, namely Master Peter Atholl, minister of the parish, a man of comely figure and gentle in his language. He sitting companionably at the side of Marian Isbister, taketh her hand into his.

ATHOLL: Thou art in miserable estate truly.

MARIAN: I am and may God help me.

ATHOLL: I am sent to thee by my masters.

MARIAN: I have told everything about myself. What more do they want me to say?

ATHOLL: They accuse thee to be guilty of corn-blighting, of intercourse with fairies, of incendiarism, the souring of ale, making butterless the milk of good kye, and much forby.

MARIAN: No witch's mark was found on me.

ATHOLL: The point of a pin is but a small thing, and thy body a large area. Here are no cunning witch-finders who would infallibly know the spot where the finger of the devil touched thee with his dark blessing.

Whereupon, Marian Isbister answering nothing, and a sign being given by Master Atholl, three men entered the prison, of whom the first unlocked the chain at her wrist, the second brought wine in a flask, and the third a lamp which he hung at the wall.

ATHOLL: This is in celebration of thy enlargement. Thou art free. Be glad now, and drink.

Then began Marian to weep for joy and to clap her hands.

MARIAN: I have never drunk wine, sir.

ATHOLL: This is from the earl himself. I will drink a little with thee.

Then they drink the wine together.

MARIAN: And am I at liberty to walk home tonight, a blameless woman?

ATHOLL: First thou shalt put thy mark to this paper.

MARIAN: I cannot read the writing on it.

ATHOLL: That matters nothing.

But Marian withdrew her hand from the parchment and let the quill fall from her fingers.

MARIAN: I fear you are little better than the other priest, and deceive me.

ATHOLL: You deceive yourself. Sign this paper, and all that will happen to thee is that thou shalt be tied to a cart and whipped through the street of Kirkwall, a small thing, and Piers the hangman is a good fellow who uses the scourge gently. But if thou art obdurate, that same Piers has strong hands to strangle thee, and a red fire to burn thee with, and a terrible eternity to dispatch thee into.

MARIAN: I wish I had never drunk thy wine. Take thy paper away.

Then was the chain put back on Marian Isbister's wrist, and the lamp darkened on the wall, and Master Peter Atholl left her, a silent man to her from that day to the day of her death.

John Glaitness cometh to her the next morning, who telleth her she must stand her trial before the King's sheriff in the hall of Newark of the Yards, that is to say, the earl's palace, on the Monday following.

MARIAN: I am content.

And she occupied herself much in the interval with apparent prayer, and the repetition of psalms, wherein she showed sharp memory for an unlettered girl.

Howbeit, she ate and drank now with relish, as one who had little more to fear or to hope for. In the days before her trial, for food she had brose, and potage, and a little fish, and milk, ale, and water for her drink, without stint.

Two days before the commencement of her trial, there came to Earl Patrick Stewart where he was hunting in Birsay, a deputation of men from her parish, among them a few who were mentioned in the indictment as having been damaged by her machinations, namely, George Taing whose butter-kirn she had enchanted, Robert Folster whose young son she had carried to the fairies on the hill, Adam Adamson whose boat she had overturned whereby two of his three sons were drowned, these and others came to the earl at the shore of Birsay, protesting that they had never at any time laid information against Marian Isbister as having harmed them or theirs, but they knew on the contrary the charge was a devised thing by Stephen Buttquoy, a factor of the earl, for that his lustful advances to the girl Marian Isbister in the byre at Howe (Stephen Buttquoy riding round the parish at that time for the collection of his lordship's rents) had gotten no encouragement. Nor had there wanted women in the parish, and a few men also, to infect the bruised pride of Stephen Buttquoy with dark suggestions concerning the girl, out of malice and envy.

This deputation the earl heard fairly and openly, and he promised to investigate their words and allegations – 'and yet,' says he, 'Master Buttquoy is my good and faithful servant, and I will not easily believe him to be guilty of such an essayed wrenching of justice. And, furthermore, the woman is in the hands of the law, whose end is equity and peace, and doubtless if she is innocent not a hair of her head will suffer.'

The day before her trial she sat long in the afternoon with Janet Bourtree.

MARIAN: It is the common thing to be first a child, and then a maiden, and then a wife, and then perhaps a widow and an old patient woman before death. But that way is not for me.

JANET: There is much grief at every milestone. A young girl cries for a lost bird. An old woman stands among six graves or seven in the kirkyard. It is best not to tarry overlong on the road.

MARIAN: Yet with John the shepherd I might have been content for a summer or two.

JANET: Yea, and I thought that with my barbarian.

Now they bring her to trial in the great hall of the palace. There sat in judgment upon her the Sheriff, Master Malachi Lorimer. The procurator was Master James Muir. Merchants and craftsmen of the town of Kirkwall, fifteen in number, sat at the jurors' table.

The officers had much ado to keep out a noisy swarm of the vulgar, as carters, alehouse keepers, ploughmen, seamen, indigents, who demanded admittance, using much violent and uproarious language in the yard outside. And though it was the earl's desire that only the more respectable sort be admitted, yet many of those others forced a way in also. (That year was much popular disorder in the islands, on account of the earl's recent decree concerning impressed labour, and the adjustment of weights and measures, whereby certain of the commonalty claimed to be much abused in their ancient rights and freedoms.)

Marian Isbister appeared and answered 'Not guilty' to the charge in a low voice. Then began Master James Muir to list against her a heavy indictment, as burning, cursing net and plough, intercourse with devil and trow, enchanting men, cows, pigs, horses, manipulation of winds in order to extract tribute from storm-bound seamen, and he declared he would bring witnesses in proof of all.

Jean Scollie, widow in Waness, witness, said Marian Isbister walked round her house three times against the sun the night before the Lammas Market, whereby her dog fell sick and died.

Oliver Spens, farmer in Congesquoy, witness, said he was on the vessel *Maribel* crossing from Hoy to Cairston, which vessel was much tossed by storm all the way, whereby all except Marian Isbister were sick and in much fear of drowning. But the said Marian Isbister said they would all doubtless come safe to the shore.

John Lyking, farmer in Clowster, witness, said his black cow would not take the bull two years. The bull was from the farm of Howe, where Marian Isbister was in service. Yet his cow at once took the bull from the farm of Redland on the far side of the hill.

Maud Sinclair, servant lass in Howe, witness, said she had a child by Robert the ploughman there, that dwined with sickness from the age of three months, and was like to die. But as soon as Marian Isbister was taken from Howe by the earl's officers, the child began to recover.

THE SHERIFF: And is thy child well now?

MAUD SINCLAIR: It is buried these six days, and never a penny did I have from Robert the ploughman, either for the lawless pleasure he had of me, nor for the bairn's nurse-fee, nor for the laying-out and burial of the body. And but that I am told to say what I do, I have no complaint against Marian Isbister, who was ever a sweet friend to me and loving to the child.

THE SHERIFF: This is idle nonsense. Step down.

Andrew Caithness, farmer in Helyatoun, witness, said he had a fire in his haystack the very day that Marian Isbister passed that way with her black shawl coming home from the kirk. None other had passed that way that day.

MARIAN: Yet I never did thee harm, Andrew, and never till today hast thou complained of me. And did not thy leaky lantern set fire to the heather on Orphir Hill that same spring?

ANDREW: It did that, Marian.

Ann St Clair, in Deepdale, witness, said she got no butter from her churn the day she reproved Marian Isbister for kissing lewdly at the end of the peatstock her son John who was shepherd at Greenay in Birsay.

William St Clair, spouse to the above, farmer in Deepdale, witness, said he was ill at ease whenever the prisoner came about the house, which lately was more than he could abide. He had lost three sheep, and his son was held from his lawful work, and one day, all his household being in the oatfield cutting, a thick rain fell upon his field that fell nowhere else in the parish, and with the rain a wind, so that his oats were much damaged. And one day when he reproved Marian Isbister for coming so much about the place after his son, he that same night and for a week following suffered much pain in the shoulder, that kept him from work and sleep.

John St Clair, son to the above, shepherd in Greenay, witness, stated that he was a man of normal lustihood, who before he met with Marian Isbister, had fathered three children on different women in the parish. Yet after he met Marian Isbister, he was unable through her enchantment to have fleshly dealings with her, though he felt deeper affection for her than for any other woman. And this he attributed to her bewitching of his members.

Margaret Gray, spinster in Blotchnie, witness, said she had known Marian Isbister to be a witch for seven years, ever since she made extracts from the juice of flowers for reddening the cheeks, eye brighteners, and sweetening of the breath.

SHERIFF: All country girls do this, do they not?

MARGARET GRAY: Yea, but Marian hath a particular art in it, and a proper skill to know the gathering-time of herbs and their true admixture.

Now the court was dismissed for eating and refreshment, and upon its reassembly the sheriff asked Master Muir whether he had many more witnesses to call.

PROCURATOR: Upwards of a score.

SHERIFF: There is already a superfluity of that kind of evidence.

Then he asks Marian Isbister whether she wishes to speak in her defence.

MARIAN: I wished to speak, and I had much to say, but the words of John St Clair have silenced my mouth.

JANET BOURTREE: A curse on him and all the liars that have infested this court this day!

On this Janet Bourtree was removed from the court by officers.

The Sheriff then made his charge to the jury.

SHERIFF: Gentlemen, I would have you to distinguish between witchcraft and other crimes that are brought before me in this court, and God knows I am fitter to try those other crimes than the supernatural crime we are dealing with here today, for they in a sense are crimes in the natural order – that is, they have some sensible material end in view – but witchcraft involves seduction of souls and entanglements of nature, so that I would rather, as in the old days, some doctor of divinity and not I were sitting solemnly on this bench. And furthermore this devil's work displays itself under an aspect of infernal roguishness, on the mean level of jugglers and conjurers, so that the dignity of this court is sorely strained dealing with it. Yet try the case we must.

Gentlemen, I have said that straightforward crime is an

ordinary enough matter. What befalls a man who steals a sheep from his neighbour? A rope is put about his neck and he is hanged; and rightly so, for by such stealing the whole economy and social harmony of the countryside is endangered. As men of property, you appreciate that.

And what becomes of a man who murders his neighbour, by knife or gun? For him also the rope is twisted and tied, and a tree of shame prepared. And rightly so, for an assassin's blade tears the whole fabric of the community. As men who uphold the sanctities of life and property, you appreciate that.

There are worse crimes still. How do we treat the man who denies the authority of his lord and seeks to overthrow it, either by cunning or by overt force? I speak not only of treason against the sovereign. There are not wanting nearer home men who murmur against the sweet person and governance of Patrick Stewart our earl.

A VOICE: When will sweet Patrick restore our ruined weights and measures? When will he leave our women alone? Sweet Patrick be damned!

At this point was taken into custody by the court officers a smallholder, Thomas Harra, who later suffered public whipping for his insolence; though many present swore that the said Thomas Harra had not once opened his mouth.

SHERIFF: You know, gentlemen, that under God we men live according to a changeless social order. Immediately under God is the King; then the lords temporal and spiritual; then knights; then craftsmen, merchants, officers, lawyers, clergymen; then at the base (though no whit less worthy in God's sight) the great multitude of fishermen, ploughmen, labourers, hewers of wood and drawers of water. Thus society appears as an organism, a harmony, with each man performing his pre-ordained task to the glory of God and the health of the whole community. He who sets himself against that harmony is worthy of a red and wretched end indeed. As loyal citizens, you appreciate that.

Such deaths we reserve for the thief, the murderer, the rebel.

Yet these criminals, though indeed they do the devil's work, are in a sense claimants on our pity, for they think, though perversely, that they are doing good. Your sheep-stealer thinks that perchance his ram could breed thick wool and fat mutton out of that grey fleece on his neighbour's hill. Your murderer undoubtedly thinks the world would be a quieter place for himself if his victim's tombstone were prematurely raised. Your rebel (God help him) hears in his mind, through pride and arrogance, a nobler social harmony than that which obtains, for example, under our God-appointed Patrick – a sweeter concourse of pipes and lutes.

A VOICE: A piper like Patrick would have his arse kicked black and blue from every ale-house in Orkney!

On this, three more men were ejected from the court room.

SHERIFF: Today we are dealing with another kind of crime altogether, namely witchcraft.

Gentlemen, you see standing before you what appears to be an innocent and chaste girl. She has a calm honest demeanour, has she not? She could be your daughter, or mine, and we would not be ashamed of her, would we? Are not your hearts moved to pity by what you see? You would hasten to succour any woman in such parlous danger of death and the fire as she is in, and yet here, in this young person, we observe a special sweetness, a unique openness of countenance, a right winning modesty.

Gentlemen, we will not allow ourselves to be led astray by appearances.

Further, you might say, 'What is this she is accused of – changing the wind, drying the dugs of an old cow, causing a lascivious youth to be chaste? Nay (you might say) these are light derisory things, and not weighty at all in the normal scale of crime.'

Yet see this thing for what it truly is.

The souls of thief, murderer, rebel are yet in the hand of

God until their last breath, but the soul of a witch is forfeit irrevocably because of the pact she has made with the Adversary.

We say this of a witch, that she is a thousand times worse than those others. She is pure evil, utter and absolute darkness, an assigned agent of hell. Of her Scripture says, *Thou shalt not suffer a witch to live.*

Regarding the apparent lightness of her misdemeanours, marvel not at that. The Prince of Darkness is not always a roaring lion, an augustitude, a harrower of the souls of men; but frequently he seeks to lure and destroy with ridiculous playful actions, like the clown or the fool at a country fair; and then, when we are convulsed with that folly, off comes the disguise, and the horn, the tail, the cloven goat hoof, the unspeakable reek of damnation, are thrust into our faces.

So, in seeming simplicity and innocence, a girl lives in her native parish. Events strange, unnatural, ridiculous, accumulate round her, too insignificant one might think to take account of. These are the first shoots of a boundless harvest of evil.

Know that evil makes slow growth in the soil of a God-ordained society. But it is well to choke the black shoots early. For if we neglect them, then in the fulness of time must we eat bitter dark bread indeed – blasphemy, adultery, fratricide, tempest, flood, war, anarchy, famine.

As men of God I ask you to consider these things, and to reach now an honest verdict in the secrecy of your chamber.

It was no long time when the jury came back with the one word *Guilty*. Then rose from his place the dempster.

DEMPSTER: Marian Isbister, for this thy crime of witchcraft proven against thee in this court, thou shalt be taken tomorrow to Gallowsha, and at the stake there strangled till no breath remains in thee, and afterwards thy body shall be burnt to ashes and scattered to the winds, and this is pronounced for doom. May the Lord have mercy on thy soul.

CHAPLAIN: Amen.

Then was Marian Isbister taken down to her prison. And at once came to her William Bourtree, Simon Leslie, John Glaitness and John Beaton, with shears, razors, and pincers, who cut off her hair and afterwards shaved her skull clean, denuding her even of her eyebrows. Then one by one with the pincers John Glaitness drew out her finger-nails and toe-nails; and this operation caused her much pain.

Then they give her water but her bleeding fingers will not hold the cup.

They put their heaviest chain upon her and left her.

That night was with her Master Andrew Monteith the chaplain, and Master Peter Atholl the parish minister, from before midnight till dawn.

MONTEITH: This is thy last night on earth.

MARIAN: I thank God for it.

Then they sought with mild comforting words to prepare her for her end. By full confession of her fault it might be God would yet have mercy on her. Yet she answered only with sighs and shakings of her head.

ATHOLL: Only say, art thou guilty of witchcraft, yea or nay.

MARIAN: It needs must be.

MONTEITH: I think the devil would not love thee now, with thy skull bare as an egg.

MARIAN: I have much pain and much sorrow.

Then they read to her from the beginning of the Book, God's marvellous creation, the happiness of Adam in the Garden, Eve's temptation by the Serpent, the eating of the fruit, the angel with the flaming sword, Abel's good sacrifice and the red hand of Cain.

To these holy words she listened with much meekness.

Then said she: 'Tell my father the sheep Peggy knows the path down to the cliff, and he is to keep watch on her to keep her from that dangerous place. And tell him there is a sleeve still to sew in his winter shirt, but Isabel his neighbour will see to that.'

Then they read to her the ending of the Book, Revelation. And having prayed, soon after dawn they left her.

In the morning, at eight o'clock, when they came for her, she was asleep. They had to rouse her with shakings and loud callings of her name.

MARIAN: It is cold.

SIMON LESLIE: Thou will soon be warm enough.

MARIAN: Yea, and there are longer fires than the brief flame at Gallowsha.

Because her toes were blue and swollen after the extraction of the cuticles, she could not walk but with much difficulty. Therefore they bound her arms and carried her out on to the street. There was much laughter and shouting at sight of her naked head. Every ale-house in town had been open since midnight, the earl having decreed a public holiday. All night people had come into the town from the parishes and islands. There was much drunkenness and dancing along the road to Gallowsha.

As she hobbled through the Laverock with her fingers like a tangle of red roots at the end of her long white arms, and her head like an egg, some had pity for her but the voices of others fell on her in a confusion of cursing and ribaldry and mockery, so that the holy words of Master Andrew Monteith could scarcely be heard.

They came to Gallowsha by a steep ascent. There beside the stake waited Piers with a new rope in his hand. With courtesy and kind words he received Marian Isbister from her jailers, and led her to the stake.

PIERS: My hands are quick at their work. Thou hast had enough of pain. Only forgive me for what I have to do.

Marian Isbister kissed him on the hands.

At this, some of the crowd shouted, 'The witch's kiss, the witch's kiss!' But Piers answered, 'I do not fear that.'

It is usual on such occasions for the sentence to be read out first, and thereafter ceremonially executed on the body of the criminal. But the clerk had not uttered three words when Piers secretly put the rope about the neck of Marian Isbister and made a quick end. Those standing near saw her give a quick shrug, and then a long shiver through her entire body. She was dead before the clerk had finished reading from the parchment. Most of that great crowd saw nothing of the strangling.

An ale booth had been erected near the stake. Men crowded in there till the walls bulged. Many were too drunk to get near the fire. To that burning came Neil the Juggler with his two dancing dogs, Firth with his fiddle and new ballad entitled 'The Just and Dreadful End of Marian Isbister for Sorcery', Richan the hell-fire preacher, the long-haired dwarf Mans with medicine to cure consumption, palsy, the seven poxes, toothache, women's moustaches, the squinnying eye – all of whom made great uproar at Gallowsha until the time of the gathering of the ashes into a brass box, and their secret removal to the summit of the hill Wideford.

That same day, in the palace of Holy Rood, Edinburgh, King James the Sixth of Scotland, acting on private information, set his seal to a paper ordering due inquiry to be instituted into alleged defalcations, extortions, oppressions, and tortures practised by his cousin Earl Patrick Stewart on the groaning inhabitants of Orkney, whereby the whole realm was put in jeopardy and the providence of God affronted.

At midnight, in the town of Kirkwall, the dancing was still going on.

MASTER HALCROW, PRIEST

An obstinate uprooted man, I write this in the Glebe of the parish of Stromness, Orkney, on a harvest evening in the year of Our Lord 1561, to make more clear in my mind the dark things that have come upon us this ten years and more, especially the dreadful thing that happened yesterday, the end and consummation of all, the final untruth. A jug of ale is at my elbow, brewed by Jean Riddach (her man is this twenty winters my servant at the Glebe and does the harvesting and ploughing). I write with a warmed body and a cold uncertain mind.

I was, until yesterday, mass-priest at Stromness in the islands. My age is near what the psalmist celebrated, seventy, that sweet secret number that opens the door into eternity. My kirk, St Peter's, is built above the rocks at the shore. My people are fishermen and crofters. A few women come to my Mass each morning, and when I confess to God at the altar, to these also I confess – I fish too long at the rock, I pray only a little, I drink too much of the dark ale that they brew on the hill.

Last winter before Yule, the canon came on his rounds. He has this living but resides in Kirkwall so that he may fulfil his duties as precentor in the Cathedral of Saint Magnus there. (My lord the bishop troubles the lonely places but little.) The canon told me there was a new queen in Scotland, out of France, Mary her name (Our Lady, pray for her). 'Bloody times,' said the canon, 'bloody days indeed, and dour stickit men in the high places of Scotland, heretics and upstarts...' And what would an old priest, one who fishes and drinks too much, know about that? I inquired no more into the matter.

The canon rode away on his mare, still wagging his head

in disapproval of the times.

Saint Peter the fisherman, pray for the Church. Our Lady of the sea, pray for the Church, that it does not shipwreck in this age. Who am I to accuse, a priest that fishes and drinks too much? (and even so I hope for a great host of cuithe to be at the rock tonight – my line is ready with six hooks and bits of whitemaa feather for lure). Yet this I must record, though I shrink from it. Magnus Anderson, curate in Sandwick, lives and eats and sleeps with a huge woman called Angela – much laughter and lewd winks and silence in the parishes on that account. Jerome Clements in Hoy (this I know for truth) has not said Mass since the Feast of the Assumption in August. In Stenness John Coghill gabbles his Latin like a duck, yet because he is bastard son to the prebend's cousin, a place therefore had needs be found for him. Saint Magnus, pray for the Church. Pray for an old man whose throat is dry, though not with praying. And pray also for the good and worthy priests that are everywhere in the islands, true guardians of the Word. Easy it is to write of wickedness; their goodness is hidden with God.

There was lately a man come to the town of Kirkwall that preached under the sky like a friar, his texts the Scarlet Woman and Anti-Christ and the Whore of Babylon out of the Apocalypse. This man was not licensed by the bishop. Yet many heard him. There was shrieking, babbling, seeing of visions and speaking in tongues. Men sobbed and declared their sins openly in the streets. The bishop took no steps to control this false pretender to primitive truth, who presently went north to the outer islands and on into Shetland. The blasphemous clowning came to an end. Yet why did this thing, while it lasted, fill me with such dread, as if it was the shadow of an immense oncoming evil?

I had nine haddocks in my hand, a cold silver bunch like a silent bell, climbing the rocks with gulls all about me, when a solitary horseman rode over Innertun into my view. (This was the time of tall green corn, before the last burnish comes upon it and the heavy ears droop.) I saw at once who this horseman was, the bishop. He had a grave white look on him. He is a priest of much learning in the tongues – Scots, Latin, Gaelic, English, French, Greek, Italian. I have heard his sermons are deep subtle utterances, things of form and beauty, but I have never been to the Cathedral Kirk of Saint Magnus since my ordination fifty years ago and so I have no knowledge of his preaching. I like a sermon to be plain and wholesome like a bannock to hungry men, such as Jerome Clements used to preach in Hoy before he ceased to say Mass and took to reading German and Swiss books.

His lordship eyed the fish and said, 'This kirk is well called Saint Peter's.' Then with much gravity he said he did not know how what he must now say would affect such an old man as myself – Master Anderson and Master Clements had heard it unmoved. 'My lord,' I said, 'in truth I fish and drink too much.'

'Leave that alone,' he said. 'I have no power over you any more.'

'You are my bishop,' I said.

'There are no bishops in Scotland now,' he said. 'The old kirk is put away. There is a new kirk in the land.'

'Old kirk?' I said. 'New kirk? I know but one Kirk, that which Our Lord founded.'

'It seems that now we must believe otherwise,' said the bishop.

'Who bids us believe otherwise?' I said. 'Is it the Pope?'

'No,' said the bishop. 'The Government of Scotland has passed a law. The Pope's authority is put down. All bishops and priests are abolished, and also the Mass. Relic and image and altar must be removed at once from our kirks. The word of God is become the sole guide. Every man will discover the truth that his own soul requires in holy scripture. Henceforth every man is his own priest.'

'The priesthood abolished?' I said. 'This is droll talk. I was told at the time of my first becoming a priest that I was a priest forever in the stream of the apostolic succession, and can any men of the temporality take this title from me? This was never told me before, your grace, either by you or by your predecessor that ordained me, may God keep his soul in peace.'

The bishop's face was a total flush from brow to chin. 'You must not call me "your grace" any more,' he said in a low voice. 'I am no more a bishop. Things are thus in Scotland now. We cannot alter it. They are powerful and angry men that rule in the land.'

There was silence between us then for a little while.

I then said that this was the only place I knew, and where would I and the other Orkney priests go?

'The new kirk,' said the bishop, 'will have need of ministers. You will be asked to bide where you are. Like enough you will have more money in your purse, and a louder voice in the ordering of the parish, and new freedoms, whereby for example celibacy will not be enforced and you will be able to take a woman in marriage.'

'The new kirk is kind to an old man who has been used to silence for fifty years,' I said with as much mockery and bitterness as I could infuse into my voice. 'Tell me, your grace, what will Master Anderson and Master Clements and Master Coghill do?'

'They have all three abandoned their priesthood,' said the bishop, 'together with most of the clergy of Orkney. They will adhere as ministers to this new kirk. Master Anderson was married this very morning to the fat woman that looks after his goats.' (This about goats I took to be a figurative expression, signifying inordinate lust, since Master Anderson has at no time kept goats.) Another brief silence fell between us.

I then asked the bishop what he himself would do, now that the wolf was in the sheepfold and the ravening had begun.

'I am not brave enough to be a martyr,' he said curtly. 'Tell me, Master Halcrow, what will you do?'

I said that I did not know. Here I was and here like enough I would sit until God's will in the matter was made plain.

Then the bishop rose to his feet and pressed my hand and left the Glebe. I have not seen him again.

Yesterday began the cutting of the oats at the Glebe. The kirk lay like a foundering ship in long windy surges of corn. The first thing I saw when I looked out at the door was John Riddach my servant sharpening his blade on a red whetstone at the end of the barn.

After Mass (the usual women were there, seven of them, with heads covered) came three strangers into the kirk, to whom I (putting out the candles) remarked that they were too late, the Mass was over for that morning, but they were welcome to bide in the kirk for as long as they liked. In truth I was anxious to get down to my boat, there being mackerel in Hoy Sound that day. 'The Mass is over,' I told them.

'The Mass is over for ever,' said one of the men.

The second man drew a writ from his pocket which I saw bore the bishop's seal. 'I am Master Esson, notary from Kirkwall,' he said, 'and this young gentleman, Master Heddle, is newly appointed minister in this reformed kirk. You are commanded to hand over the keys to him at once.'

'The Mass is damnable idolatry,' said the third man in a familiar voice. I looked closer at him, and behold it was Magnus Anderson the Sandwick priest, the same which had kept the woman Angela in concubinage five years and was now her unsanctified spouse.

I then said very tartly to Master Anderson that he had been a long time finding out that the Mass was (as he termed it) damnable idolatry, and then, the sharpness increasing in my voice, I took leave to congratulate with him upon his new estate of matrimony, which was indeed a singular state for a man who had sworn before God to observe lifelong chastity.

I turned then to the other men and said that the keys were in my keeping and I would never give them over unless by order of the bishop. Then they showed me the bishop's writ, with his commands and wishes clearly set out. Thereupon with no more ado I made over the keys to them.

They waited for me to leave the kirk.

I bade them look well to the building, for it was a place dear to me, I having been a priest here fifty years until now. Every stone was become precious to me. Some of the stones on the pavement are from the beach, I told them, and these stones shine with wetness like dark mirrors when there is a dampness in the atmosphere, for then those stones (as it seems) remember the element of water out of which they have been taken. And yet, I said, great pity it were to remove these stones, for so lying juxtaposed with the dry stones from the quarry, they seemed to show forth the intertwining elements in this parish, sea and soil, the fish and the cornstalk, and indeed Saint Peter our patron had himself been a fisherman who doubtless often came wet from the sea to his prayers. And did not the very name Peter mean stone, permanence, unassailability?

Doubtless I would have spoken much more, to gather my squandered senses and delay my expulsion from the place, but Master Magnus Anderson turned to his companions and remarked anent me, 'This one always was and ever will be to his dying day a garrulous long-winded old man. Once launched on some topic like sillock-fishing or the five various ways of brewing ale, he becomes a weariness of the flesh.'

On this, there stirred in me and roused itself and presently raged that third beast of hell among the seven beasts, Wrath, and I said to Master Magnus Anderson directly concerning his long entertaining of the sixth beast of hell, Lust, (yet never does one beast cancel out another, and herein I erred grievously) – 'I trust that Mistress Angela is well,' I said. 'She is an immense piece of territory, your Newfoundland, but doubtless in time you will be able to chart the geography of her to your satisfaction, and wring much fruitfulness out of her, Father.'

He who now had charge of the parish, the new minister, fearing violence, came between us and said beseechingly that now it was time for me to go.

Thereupon I bowed my knee to the altar where lay the Body of Our Lord and turned my back on those men and left the kirk.

I walked along the coast with a blank beating mind, having now no secure place in the world, for certain it seemed to me that they would take from me also the Glebe and my furrows and boat. Near noon I sat down near the edge of the cliff (called the Black Craig) to rest me. There the seabirds circled and fell, gleaning the waves for food. Now came this fragment of the Word into my mind, that had been the Gospel of the Sunday preceding:

Behold the birds of the air, for they neither sow, nor do they reap, nor gather into barns, and your heavenly Father feedeth them. Are not you of much more value than they?

And scarcely the last word was remembered when this desolation came suddenly into my mind, a thing I had clean forgot in the kirk in my rage and grief – the *Blessed Sacrament*! What might such men do to the Bread of Heaven, seeing that for them now it was no longer the Body of Our Lord but mortal bread over which five invalid words had been uttered?

I turned back over the fields, taking the bird's path to the kirk. Yet it was not like a bird that I went, rather it was like an old wounded beast, hard beset, that groaned and laboured under the yoke. John Riddach was in the oatfield, making bright circles with his scythe. And presently, the last breath it seemed guttering in my mouth, I came again to the kirk and went in at the door.

There a shameful thing had been done. They had thrown down the statues of Our Lady and Saint Peter and Saint Magnus. The crucifix lay broken at the base of the font (agony upon agony). The stones were pale with smashed candles. I looked wildly round for the white circles of the Host to be scattered about the place but (thanks be to God!) there was no such thing, though the tabernacle stood open.

The notary shouted, 'That one is back again, the old windbag is back! Were you not well admonished to quit this place for ever? Have you not wrought disgrace enough in this place, with your drunkenness and your idleness?'

'Not to speak of his idolatry and blasphemy,' said Angela's man.

The young minister, my successor (yet where was the succession? it was rather a total uprooting) said in a voice that was all delusive hope, 'It may be that Master Halcrow wishes to join our congregation. That would be a thing pleasing to us all.'

'No,' I said. 'I wish to speak with this priest, Master Anderson.'

'There is no such thing as priest any more,' said the lawyer. 'Give him his proper title.'

'Say quickly what you want,' said Master Magnus Anderson. 'Here I am.'

'I must speak with you alone,' I said.

Master Anderson shuffled his feet and looked uneasily about him, like a dog that hears contrary orders and does not well understand either the one or the other, or where to turn his head.

Then after a short consideration the young minister said, 'You can have private talk with him for as long as it takes to utter a short psalm.' Thereupon he took the lawyer by the arm and both left by the front door, the lawyer looking back over his shoulder very ill-pleased.

I said quickly to Master Anderson, 'The Blessed Sacrament.'

Master Anderson smiled. He opened his coat. He drew from an inner pocket the bright pyx. With trembling hands he put It into my trembling hand. Then he bent forward and kissed me on the cheek. 'Pray for me, Master Halcrow,' he said. 'Pray for me. I was intending to consume It myself.'

'I will, Magnus,' I said, 'both before and after my death...' Then I spoke with him briefly concerning my death. 'I feel the ripeness and the rot of it inside me,' I said. 'I beg that you will come to me with the oil when you hear that I am on my last bed, either openly or in secret.'

We heard the returning shuffle of feet at the door.

'I will come in secret,' said Master Anderson.

The lawyer came back first into the kirk.

I said in a loud voice, 'I much regret what I said earlier concerning Mistress Anderson. Every body, however gross, is a temple of the Holy Ghost, and I did ill to describe it in those obscene terms.'

Master Anderson gave a bitter smile. The minister came back into the kirk. The lawyer said, 'Go now. We have much work to do in this place before it is a fit temple of the Lord and no more a temple of Baal.'

I turned my back on them – *Domine, non sum dignus* – and I put the round white circles of the Host into my mouth.

Thus transfixed, I crossed myself and walked out of the kirk. The stooks were rising bright in every field. There were two fishing boats off the Graemsay rocks. Jean Riddach was at the well with her bucket.

Saint Peter, pray for us.

THE STORY OF JORKEL HAYFORKS

THE week before midsummer Jorkel and six others took ship at Bergen in Norway and sailed west two days with a good wind behind them. They made land at Whalsay in Shetland and were well entertained at a farm there by a man called Veig. After they had had supper one of Jorkel's men played the harp and recited some verses. The name of this poet was Finn.

As soon as Finn had sat down, Brenda, the daughter of Veig the Shetlander, came to her father and said, 'Offer Finn a horse and a piece of land, so that he will be pleased to stay here.'

Veig made the offer to Finn, but Finn said, 'We are sailing to Orkney on a certain urgent matter in the morning. I can't stay.'

Veig repeated Finn's remark to Brenda.

At midnight when the men were drinking round the fire, Brenda rose out of bed and said to her father Veig, 'I can't get to sleep. Offer Finn a gold arm-band and a silver ring to stay here in Shetland.'

Veig called Finn aside and made this offer. Finn said, 'I am a poor man and a happy man, and gold and women would distract me from the making of verses. Besides, we have an appointment to keep in Orkney on midsummer day.'

Veig told Brenda what Finn had said.

At dawn, though the ale keg was empty, the men were still sitting at the fire. Some of them were lying under the benches drunk, but Finn was discussing metres with the Shetlanders. 'I would argue better,' said Finn, 'if I was not so dry.'

Soon after that Brenda came in and offered Finn a cup of ale.

With the froth still wet on his beard, Finn turned to Brenda and said, 'Did you brew this ale, woman?' Brenda said that she alone had made it. Then Finn said, 'On account of this ale I will stay for a while with you here in Shetland.'

Then the sun got up and the Norwegians stirred themselves and went on board their ship. But Finn was nowhere to be found, and the door of Brenda's room was barred. Jorkel was very angry about that.

They say that Finn made no more poems after that day. Brenda bore him twelve children. He died there in Shetland before there was a grey hair in his beard. He was drunk most days till his death, and he would drink from no cup but Brenda's. He was totally dependent on her always. It was thought rather a pity that such a promising poet should make such an ordinary end.

'She bewitched him, that bitch,' said Jorkel.

In the afternoon of the same day, Jorkel's ship reached Fair Isle. They saw some sheep on a hillside there. Flan, who was a blacksmith back in Norway, said they were fine sheep. 'And my wife,' said he, 'will be looking for a present from the west. I will bring her a fleece from Fair Isle.'

Before they could stop Flan he leapt overboard and swam ashore. The sheep were grazing at the edge of a high cliff. Flan climbed up this face, disturbing the sea birds that were there, and laid hands on the first sheep he saw. He was raising his axe to despatch the ewe when another sheep ran terrified between his legs and toppled him over the edge of the crag, so that the sea birds were wildly agitated for the second time that day.

'Flan's descent is much quicker than his going up,' said Jorkel. 'What does a blacksmith know about shepherding?'

They anchored that night under the cliffs of Fair Isle.

They left Fair Isle at dawn and had a rough crossing to the Orkneys. There was a strong wind from the east and the sea fell into the ship in cold grey lumps, so that they were kept busy with the bailing pans.

Then Mund who had a farm east in Sweden laid down his bailing pan.

He said, 'I have made deep furrows in the land with my plough but I did not believe there could be furrows in the world like this.'

The men went on bailing.

Later Mund said, 'When Grettir lay dying in his bed at Gothenburg last summer his face was like milk. Is my face that colour?'

Jorkel said his face was more of a green colour, and urged the men to bail all the harder, since now Mund was taking no part in the game.

At noon Mund said, 'I was always a gay man at midsummer, but I do not expect to be dancing round a Johnsmas fire this year.'

The men went on bailing, until presently the wind shifted into the north and moderated, so that they were able to cook a meal of stewed rabbit and to open a keg of ale.

But when they brought the meat and ale to Mund, they found him lying very still and cold against a thwart.

'Mund will not be needing dinner any more,' said Jorkel.

They reached Papa Westray soon after that. There were some decent farms in the island, and an ale-house near the shore, and a small monastery with a dozen bald-headed brothers beside a loch.

The people of the island gave them a hospitable welcome, and sold them fish and mutton, and showed them where the best wells were.

The twelve brothers trooped into the church for vespers.

After the necessary business of victualling had been transacted, the Norwegians went into the ale-house to drink.

They played draughts and sang choruses so long as there

was ale in the barrel. Then, when the keeper of the ale-house was opening a new barrel, Jorkel noticed that Thord was missing.

'He will have gone after the women of Papa Westray,' said Sweyn. Thord was known to be a great lecher back home in Norway.

The church bell rang for compline.

There was some fighting in the ale-house when they were midway through the second barrel, but by that time they were too drunk to hurt each other much. When things had quietened down, Jorkel remarked that Thord was still absent.

'No doubt he is stealing eggs and cheese, so that we can vary our diet on the ship,' said Valt. Thord was a famous thief on the hills of southern Norway, when it was night and everyone was sitting round the fires inside and there was no moon.

They went on drinking till the lights of yesterday and tomorrow met in a brief twilight and their senses were reeling with ale and fatigue.

'This is a strange voyage,' said Jorkel. 'It seems we are to lose a man at every station of the way.'

They heard the bell of the church ringing. Jorkel went to the door of the ale-house. Thirteen hooded figures passed under the arch to sing matins.

Jorkel returned to the ale barrel and said, 'It seems that Thord has repented of his drinking and whoring and thieving. Yesterday there were twelve holy men in Papa Westray. This morning I counted thirteen.'

He lay down beside his companions, and they slept late into the morning.

Now there were only three men on the ship, Jorkel and Sweyn and Valt.

'We will not stop until we reach Hoy,' said Jorkel. 'Every time we stop there is one kind of trouble or another.'

They were among the northern Orkneys now, sailing through a wide firth with islands all around.

It turned out that none of the three knew where exactly Hoy was.

Sweyn said, 'There is a man in that low island over there. He has a mask on and he is taking honey from his hives. I will go ashore and ask him where Hoy is.'

'Be careful,' said Jorkel. 'We will have difficulty in getting to Hoy if there are only two of us left to work the ship.'

Sweyn waded ashore and said to the bee-keeper, 'Be good enough to tell us how we can recognize the island of Hoy.'

The man took off his mask and replied courteously that they would have to sail west between the islands until they reached the open ocean, and then keeping the coast of Hrossey on the port side and sailing south they would see in the distance two blue hills rising out of the sea. These blue hills were Hoy.

Sweyn thanked him and asked if he was getting plenty of honey.

The man replied that it was a bad year for honey. The bees had been as dull as the weather.

'Still,' the bee-keeper said, 'the next comb I take from the hive will be a gift for you.'

Sweyn was deeply touched by the courtesy and kindness of the bee-keeper.

It happened that as the man was bending over the hive, a bee came on the wind and settled on his neck and stung him.

The bee-keeper gave a cry of annoyance and shook off the bee.

Sweyn was angry at the way the insects repaid with ingratitude the gentleness of the Orkney bee-keeper. He suddenly brought his axe down on the hive and clove it in two.

Jorkel and Valt were watching from the ship, and they saw Sweyn run screaming round the island with a cloud of bees after him. It was as if he was being pelted with hot sharp sonorous hail stones.

36

Sweyn ran down into the ebb and covered himself with seaweed.

When Jorkel and Valt reached him, he told them where Hoy was. Then his face turned blind and blue and swollen and he died.

Jorkel and Valt got horses at a farm called the Bu in Hoy and rode between the two hills till they came to a place called Rackwick. There was a farm there and five men were working in the hayfield. It was a warm bright day, and the faces of the labourers shone with sweat.

Jorkel asked them if a man called Arkol lived nearby.

'Arkol is the grieve at this farm,' said one of the labourers, 'but he often sleeps late.'

'We work in the daytime,' said another, 'but Arkol does most of his labouring at night.'

'Arkol is a great man for the women,' said a third, and winked.

Jorkel said he thought that would be the man they were looking for.

Presently the labourers stopped to rest and they invited Jorkel and Valt to share their bread and ale. They sat under a wall where there was shadow and Valt told all that had happened to them from the time they left Bergen. But Jorkel sat quietly and seemed preoccupied. They noticed too that he did not eat or drink much.

'Who is the owner of this farm?' said Valt when he had finished his story of the voyage.

The labourers said the farmer in Rackwick was a man called John. They spoke highly of him. He was a good master to them.

Just then a man with a dark beard crossed the field. He ordered the labourers to resume their work, and then looked suspiciously at Jorkel and Valt. They were rather scruffy and dirty after their voyage.

Jorkel asked him if his name was Arkol Dagson.

The man yawned once or twice and said that it was.

'In that case,' said Jorkel, 'I must tell you that my sister Ingirid in Bergen bore you a son at the beginning of June.'

Arkol made no answer but yawned again. Then he laughed.

'And I want to know,' said Jorkel, 'if you will pay for the fostering of the child.'

Arkol said he would not discuss so intimate a matter with two tramps. So far he had not been in the habit of paying for the fostering of any child that he had fathered, and he doubted whether it was wise to begin now, especially as Norway was so far away. Furthermore, he could hardly be expected to believe the unsupported testimony of two tramps, one of whom claimed to be Ingirid's brother. Ingirid had been a most lovely and gently-reared girl, and Arkol did not think the scarecrow standing before him could really be the brother of such a delightful bedmate. Besides, he had been busy all night in another sweet bed, and now he was very tired, and he begged the two gentlemen of the roads to excuse him.

Jorkel said, 'Will you pay now for the fostering of your son?'

Arkol turned away and yawned.

Jorkel drove his dagger into Arkol's throat, so that he fell dead at once on the field.

The labourers jumped down from the haystack and ran at Jorkel and Valt with their forks.

'I wish the others were here now,' said Jorkel as he turned to face them. 'Now I would be glad to have Finn and Flan and Mund and Thord and Sweyn at my side.'

Valt was quickly pronged to death there, and though Jorkel defended himself well and was still on his feet when John of Rackwick appeared on the scene, he was so severely lacerated that he lay between life and death in the farm for more than a week.

The three farm girls looked after him well till he recovered. They hovered around him day and night with oil and sweet water and beeswax.

On the day they took the last bandages from Jorkel's arm, John of Rackwick came to him and said mildly, 'Arkol, my grieve, was in many ways an evil lecherous man, and for that he must answer to a higher lord than the Earl of Orkney or the King of Norway. But also he was a loyal servant of mine, and because of that you must pay me as compensation your ship that is anchored off Selwick. You are welcome to stay here in Hoy, Jorkel, for as long as you like. There is a small vacant croft on the side of the hill that will support a cow and an ox and a few sheep. It will be a tame life for a young man, but now you are disabled because of the hay forks, and if you till your field carefully nothing could be more pleasing to God.'

Jorkel accepted that offer. He lived there at Upland for the rest of his life. In Orkney he was nicknamed 'Hayforks'. He put by a little money each harvest so that one day he would be able to return to Norway, but the years passed and he could never get a passage.

The summer before his death Jorkel went to Papa Westray in a fishing boat. At the church there he inquired for Thord, and presently Thord came out to meet him. They were two old men now, bald and toothless. They embraced each other under the arch. They were like two boys laughing to each other over an immense distance, thin affectionate lost voices.

Jorkel took a purse from his belt and counted five pieces of silver into Thord's hand. 'I have been saving this money for forty years,' he said, 'so that some day I could go home to Norway. But it is too late. Who would know me in Bergen now? I should prepare, instead, for the last, longest journey. Will you arrange for masses to be said in your church for Finn and Flan and Mund and Sweyn and Valt?'

Thord said that masses would certainly be offered for those dead men and for Jorkel himself too. Then he embraced Jorkel and blessed him. Jorkel turned round. He was at peace. The long silver scars of the hayforks troubled his body no longer.

Half-way to the boat he turned back. He gave Thord another silver coin. 'Say a mass for Arkol Dagson also,' he said. They smiled at each other, crinkling their old eyes.

A TIME TO KEEP

I

WE came down through the fields, Ingi and I.

The wedding was still going on in her father's house in Osmundwall, ten miles over the hill.

There were lacings of snow across the valley and the upper hills were white.

We saw our house in front of us, a clean new house of sea-washed stones. There was no earth-weathering on the walls yet. I had built the house myself between harvest and Christmas. Fires had been lit to burn the dampness out of it, but there was no fire yet for food and companionship. Beside the dwelling-house were byre and barn and stable that the mason had built the winter before. The thatch on the four roofs was new springy heather, covered with wire-netting and weighted with stones.

Ingi went alone into the house. I went into the byre to see that the two cows were all right. There was a sheep here and a sheep there on the field above, seven sheep in all on the hill. One sheep wandered across a line of snow, gray against white.

A new plough leaned against the wall of the barn. The blacksmith must have delivered it that afternoon. I took it inside, a gray powerful curve.

This was our croft, Ingi's and mine. I turned back towards the house. Blue smoke was rising from the roof now. The first true fire had been lit.

2

I was in the firth most days that month, though it was winter. My boat was new also. I had made her with my own hands in the month of June, the dry bright month when work can be carried on late into the night, after the croft work is over. I called the boat *Susanna* after the laird's wife, a red-faced generous woman. I thought a name like that would bring us luck.

I generally got up as soon as it was light. I left Ingi in our bed and I ate a piece of bannock and drank a mouthful of ale. Then I put on my sea-boots and my woollen cap and went down to the beach.

The other crofters who were fishermen also were always there before me that winter, and they kept apart from me. I was like a stranger in the valley.

I launched *Susanna* alone. I rowed her out into the firth alone. I set my lines alone. I didn't feel the need of anyone except Ingi.

That winter the other crofter-fishermen avoided me. Neither the old ones nor the young unmarried ones came near me. They had liked me well enough the summer before but now, since the marriage, I was, it seemed, unpopular. The men of Two-Waters especially kept to their own side of the bay.

I fished alone.

And alone I carried the haddocks up over the fields to the croft. Always the smoke was rising out of the roof, sometimes gray smoke, sometimes blue, sometimes black. But the flame beat in the hearth, the house was alive. And always when I reached the door Ingi stood there before me.

3

One night there was a storm from the south. None of the boats was in the firth next morning. The clouds pressed on the face of the hills and it was too wet to plough, though it was the time of ploughing.

I lay long in the box-bed, my face to the wall. Ingi was up soon after it was light.

I heard her going about her work. Her poker stirred a new flame out of the embers in the hearth. The door opened. She came in with her apron full of peats. The door opened again. Now she was carrying pails of new water from the burn. They rang like bells as she set them down on the flagstones. She turned some fish that were smoking in the chimney. Then her small fists beat on the table as she kneaded the dough. She poured water into a black pot. And the door kept slamming against the wall as she went out and in, louder because of the storm. 'For God's sake,' I said, 'be quiet.'

I fell asleep for a while then.

When I woke up the storm was still prowling about the house. But the door was shut tight and the house was warm and full of the smells of new bannocks and boiled fish.

'Get up,' Ingi said, 'or we'll eat up everything, the dog and myself. You've been sleeping a night and a day.' She said a small quiet prayer over the food.

Ingi and I sat at the table and ate. She had not yet learned to cook properly – the fish was raw and the bannocks full of soda. She had been busy at more than food while I was sleeping. The stone floor was still half wet from her scrubbing and she had tried to mend the four broken creels with twine. Ingi was not a valley girl. She had spent her life behind the counter of her father's shop in Osmundwall, but she was doing her best to please me. It grew dark while we were eating.

Ingi put down her bread and took a box of matches from the mantelpiece and lit the paraffin lamp. The flame came up squint – she still didn't know how to trim a wick.

We dipped the last of our bread in the fish brew. 'I hope this gale doesn't last,' said Ingi. 'Our fish is nearly done.'

The flame sank in the hearth.

'Tomorrow,' said Ingi, 'I will make ale, though I've never made it before. There isn't much malt left either. And I'll tell you what I need badly, a pair of black shoes for the kirk on Sundays.'

I rose from my chair and blew out the lamp.

Outside the storm prowled between the sea and the hills, restless as a beast.

Ingi put a black peat over the red embers so that the fire would stay alive till morning.

We leaned towards each other then and kissed in the darkness.

4

I dug out a new field at the side of the house – because no-one on God's earth could plough such a wilderness – and all the while I was tearing up stones and clumps of heather I thought to myself, 'What a fool! Sure as hell the laird will raise your rent for this day's work.' And my spade rang against stones or sank with a squelch into a sudden bit of bog.

I looked up once and saw a dozen women trooping across the fields to the school.

It was Good Friday.

I looked up another time and saw a horseman riding between the hills. It was the laird. He turned his horse towards the school also. The Easter service was being held there.

Two of my lambs had been born dead that morning. They lay, red bits of rag, under the wall. I would bury them afterwards.

There was one stone in the new field that just showed a gray curve through the heather. I took the biggest hammer in the barn and was an hour breaking it up and tearing the sharp bits out of the ground.

That was enough labour for one day. The sun was going down. I turned for home.

Ingi was not in. The house was dead. The pot sat black upon a black fire. My shoulders ached with the misery and foolishness of increasing my own rent. I was very hungry too.

Ingi was at the service with the laird and the other women, listening to the story of the lash and the whins and the nails and the last words. All the women were there sitting before the missionary with open mouths, listening to that fairy tale. I and a few others in the island knew better. Mr Simpson, B.Sc., from Glasgow had not been our schoolmaster four winters for nothing.

I spent the rest of that day in the ale-house with half a dozen other ploughmen.

And how I got home to the croft again I do not know. I woke up in the morning on the rack of my own bed, with all my clothes on.

There was a jam jar with new daffodils in it in the window.

Ingi heard my awakening, a groan and a creak.

She rose up quickly from the chair where she was peeling potatoes and put her cold hand on my forehead. 'You'll be fine now,' she said. 'Bella had two lambs in the night, such bonny peedie things! Your throat must be dry. I'll get you some water.'

Bella was the old ewe. None of her lambs, so I had been told when I bought her, ever died.

'You listen to me,' I said to Ingi. 'You spend too much money every Wednesday at that grocery van. Don't you buy any more jars of jam, and sponge cakes from the bake-house in Hamnavoe. We're poor people. Remember that.'

The daffodils in the window were like a dozen old women shawled in brightness.

The fire burned high in the hearth and the kettle sang.

I closed my eyes.

5

The old field was ploughed and the new field was completely drained and dug. When I turned for home gray smoke was rising over the chimney-head.

There were eleven sheep on the hill now and three cattle in the field, the two cows and a small black bull calf. I went into the house and Ingi was emptying the new ale out of the kirn into stone jars. 'You'll bide at home after this,' Ingi said. 'No more of that ale-house.'

But the stuff was flat. She hadn't yet mastered the craft of brewing. Until she did I would have to keep visiting the ale-house.

One day I would come in from the firth with lobsters and another day with haddocks. I got two huge halibut one morning that I could hardly carry up over the fields. She was ready with the stone jar of salt and the knife in the threshold.

I walked between the hills to pay the rent on term day. 'You've broken out land,' said the factor, 'and therefore I think it only fair you should pay ten shillings more rent come Martinmas. Furthermore you have no right to graze sheep on the hill without permission from the laird, who is not giving his permission this year. See to it.'

'Did you never hear of the Crofters' Act of 1888?' I said.

He gave me a black look. Then he licked a stamp and thudded it on the receipt and signed his name across it. 'You'll be hearing from the lawyer in Hamnavoe,' he said.

I had more kindness than usual from Ingi when I got back from that interview.

And every Sabbath she would be at the holy meeting with the old women. She was away all morning, while I sat at home reading *The Martyrdom of Man*, one of the six books in the cupboard (not counting the bible). And after the service she would come in at the door and sit in her black clothes in the chair at the other side of the fire and she would say, 'We should be very thankful.'. . . 'But,' she said one Sunday, 'my shoes are not fit to be seen in God's house.'

We were at the peat cutting a whole day that month. We came home stung with clegs, blistered by the sun, and too sore to eat or to make love. But one thing was sure: the red heart of the house would beat all next winter, for we had a great hoard of peats scattered over the hillside to dry. Ingi kissed me once and then I went to sleep in the chair till morning.

I sowed the field with oats. Then I went home in the twilight to bread and ale and the warm fire. There was a little improvement in her brewing, but still the stuff was too thick and sweet.

One morning Ingi was very sick.

6

I was sorting my catch on the beach and so were all the other fishermen when Peter of Two-Waters walked across the stones to me. John and Howie his two sons were behind him. Anna his daughter hovered in the background. 'You hauled some of my lobster creels,' Peter of Two-Waters said.

'I did not,' I said.

'Under the Kame you hauled a dozen lobster creels belonging to me,' said Peter of Two-Waters.

'That's not true,' I said.

'Don't do it again,' said Peter of Two-Waters. 'That's thieving. In Kirkwall there's a court and a sheriff and a jail.'

'I'm not a thief,' I said, 'but you're a liar.'

'Don't call my father a liar,' said John of Two-Waters. 'If you call my father a liar again I'll smash you. I will.'

'Careful,' said Howie of Two-Waters to John. Howie had always been my friend. We had sat together at the same desk in the school and afterwards we had fished together a few times and we had got drunk in each other's company in the ale-house. 'Careful now,' said Howie to his brother.

'Somebody has been hauling my creels,' said old Peter of Two-Waters. 'There'll be trouble unless it stops.'

'I fish my own lobsters,' I said.

Then I put my basket of fish on my shoulder and walked home.

The truth is, I had good catches of lobster that summer, and I shipped them to Billingsgate and got good money for them. I was at home on the sea. Everything I did there was right.

The men of Two-Waters, on the other hand, were poor fishermen. They were good enough crofters but old women could have fished better. They should never have gone on the sea. They hardly knew the bow of a yawl from the stern. The weather made them nervous too – they kept near the shore if there was one cloud in the sky or a whisper of wind.

'No,' said Ingi when I got home, 'you are not a thief. But don't get into any fights. That Howie of Two-Waters is so strong, he could kill an ox. Besides that, Anna of Two-Waters is my best friend in this valley, and I don't want there to be any trouble between us. This valley is too small for bad blood.'

She blew up the fire to heat a pot of ale. Then she knelt and drew off my sea boots.

7

I was baiting a line with mussels at the end of the house when I saw the black car coming between the hills and stopping where the road ended at the mouth of the valley. It was the first car ever seen in the island, a Ford.

A small, neat man with a beard and a watch-chain across his belly got out and came stepping briskly up our side of the valley.

'Ingi,' I shouted, 'your father's here.'

She was baking, going between the table, the cupboard, and the fire, a blue reek all about her.

But now all thought of bread was forgotten. She let out a cry of distress. She threw off her mealy apron, she filled a bowl of water and dipped face and hands in it and wiped herself dry with the towel. She put the text straight on the wall. She covered my six rationalist books with a cloth. She fell to combing her hair and twisting it into a new bright knot at the back of her head. All the same, the house was full of the blue hot reek of baking. And the bed was unmade. And

48

there was a litter of fish-guts and crab toes about the door.
She tried hard, Ingi, but she was not the tidiest of the croft
women.

Ingi came and stood at the door.

As for me, I went on with my lines. I was not beholden to
him.

Mr Sinclair, merchant in Osmundwall – and forby kirk
elder, Justice of the Peace, chairman of the district council –
stood at the corner of the barn.

'Father,' said Ingi.

'My girl,' said Mr Sinclair. He touched her gently on the
arm.

'Well, Bill,' he said to me.

'Well,' I said.

'Father, I'm glad to see you,' said Ingi.

'No happier than I am to see you,' said Mr Sinclair. 'Ingi,'
said he, 'you're not looking well. Not at all well. What way
is it that we haven't seen you for three whole months, eh?
Ingi, I doubt you're working too hard, is that it?'

'On a croft,' I said, 'everybody must work.'

'Is that so, Bill?' said Mr Sinclair. 'Maybe so. At the present
moment I'm speaking to Ingi, to my daughter. I'll be wanting
to speak to you later, before I go.'

'Say what you have to say now,' I said, 'for I have work to do.'

'Bill,' said Ingi unhappily.

'Work to do, is that it, work to do,' said Mr Sinclair. 'Then
if you have so much work to do, why don't you give my daughter
enough money for her to live on? Eh? Just answer me. Why
don't you do that? Last month you cut down on her money.
The van man told me. She couldn't buy jam or paraffin.
Don't imagine I don't hear things.'

'Father,' said Ingi. 'Please.'

'We have debts,' I said, 'to the mason for the barn and
to the fishmonger for twine and oilskins and to the dealer in
Hamnavoe for the seven sheep and the two cows. The laird,

your friend and fellow elder, is threatening to raise our rent. There was furniture and implements to pay for.'

'You and Ingi had a hundred pounds from me the week before you married,' said Mr Sinclair quietly. 'One hundred pounds sterling, a cheque for that amount.'

'You'll get it back,' I said, 'every penny.'

'Bill,' said Ingi. 'Father.'

'It was a present,' said Mr Sinclair, 'to see my daughter through her first year or two in comfort. Yes, in the kind of comfort she was used to before she came to this place. Ingi is not a strong girl. She needs looking after.'

'All the same,' I said, 'you'll be paid back. Ingi and I, we don't want your money.'

'I think we should go inside,' said Mr Sinclair. 'The whole valley's listening to what we say.'

It was true enough. A half-dozen old women were at the end of their houses, waiting like hens for scraps of scandal.

'Let them listen,' I said. 'The truth never hurt anybody.'

'Yes, come inside, *please*,' said Ingi.

'No,' I said. 'Can't you see I'm working? I must bait this line and get the boat out before the tide turns.'

'Very well,' said Mr Sinclair, 'the truth as you say will bear hearing wherever it's uttered. There are other matters to be discussed besides.'

Ingi went inside, covering her eyes with the new apron she had put on in honour of her father's arrival. From time to time I could hear a slow hard sob from inside the house.

'For example,' Mr Sinclair said, 'it has come to my ears that hardly a night passes but you're in the ale-house. Hardly a night. Yes. The ale-house. But when are you seen at the Sunday service? Never once. No, but in the ale-house when you have a few drams in you there's nothing too vile for you to say against God and his holy bible. I did not think I was marrying my daughter to a drunkard and an atheist.'

I went on baiting my line. I could hear Ingi crying continuously inside the house.

'Listen to her, the poor girl,' said Mr Sinclair. 'She does well to cry. For Ingibiorg Sinclair was a happy girl before she met up with the likes of you. She was that. And look at the shame and the misery and the poverty you've brought on her. I got her letter. She's a very unhappy girl.'

I opened a few more mussels with my knife.

'I've come here today,' he said, 'to take her home where she'll be looked after.'

I never answered.

I heard him stumping into the house. I went on with the baiting. Coil by coil the haddock line was baited. They spoke low and urgently to each other inside. Ten minutes passed. The half-dozen old women still stood at the end of the crofts. I opened a score of mussels and threw the empty blue shells on the grass among the buttercups. The gulls that had been standing along the shore all morning stirred themselves and rose seawards in tumult upon tumult of yelling circles. Down at the rock Howie of Two-Waters was stowing his creels on board. (The fool – it was not a lobster day.) I heard the door opening and a small sob out of Ingi and the brisk feet of Mr Sinclair on the threshold.

'You haven't heard the last of this,' he shouted to me.

'There's never an end to anything,' I said, 'and it's a fine morning for the haddocks.'

I waited till I heard the black Ford coughing among the hills and all the old women were inside and the last hook was baited and coiled. Then I rose and went in through the door.

Ingi sat among the half-baked bannocks, dabbing her eyes.

'Ingi,' I said, 'here's what you're going to get, a pair of new black shoes and a coat and a hat for the kirk on Sabbath. We're going to Hamnavoe on the Saturday boat, the two of us, to the shops.'

8

A new wave fell into the *Susanna* and kept the score of dying haddocks alive.

I was trying to get home before the day got worse.

It had been a fine morning. I had left Ingi in bed before the sun rose and eaten my bannock and ale standing. Then I put on thigh boots and put the oilskin over my arm.

There was sun and a blue sea when I got to the beach. The other fishermen were there too, busy around their boats. 'First the haddocks,' I said to myself, 'then the lobsters as I come home in the afternoon.'

The gulls encouraged us, white congregations drifting out in the firth, circling and dipping and crying.

I set a line and looked back at the valley. It was like a green open hand among the hills. The cliffs stood near and far, red, gray, black. In the valley chimneys began to smoke, one of them mine. Ingi was up. A green offering hand, our valley, corn-giver, fire-giver, water-giver, keeper of men and beasts. The other hand that fed us was this blue hand of the sea, which was treacherous, which had claws to it, which took more than ever it gave. Today it was peaceable enough. Blue hand and green hand lay together, like praying, in the summer dawn.

I drew in a score of haddocks, middling things.

I felt hungry after that, and had a few corn-beef sandwiches and a flask of milk.

Time for the lobsters.

I found myself drifting among three strange boats. They were Highland fishermen, from Sutherlandshire on the opposite shore of the firth. They shouted to me in Gaelic. I shook my head. One of them waved a bottle of whisky. 'This will be a language that you will be understanding,' he said in English. We drifted together. I took the bottle and had a dram. 'Another,' they said. Once more bottle and head tilted at their different angles and my throat burned. 'Ah,' said an old Highlandman, 'but you Orkneymen are terrible ones for the strong drink. Tell me,' he said, 'are they still making whisky up among the Orkney hills?' 'A few,' I said, 'but it's dangerous.' 'Ah, now,' said the old man, 'that is the real whisky, water of life, and could a man get that stuff to drink every day from the day of his weaning he would live forever.' 'I drank it once,' I said, 'and it nearly killed me.' 'People are made different,' said the old man; 'to me now it is like mother's milk.'

'I wish, however,' said a young red-headed man, 'that you Orkneymen would stay more to your own side of the firth and not poach in our waters.' 'The sea is free,' I said. 'No,' said another tall man, 'but you take our fish.' This last man who had spoken was drunk and I didn't care for the look of him, the black smoulder in his eyes when he spoke to me. 'Just as,' he went on, 'in the old days you Orkneymen came to our place and took our sheep away and were a trouble to our women. . . .' Then he said something in Gaelic which I took to be an insult. Some of the other fishermen laughed. The old man held up his hand and said, 'That is an old story that should be forgotten. It is true enough, God made the sea for all men and he created all men to be brothers. There should be no more talk of sheep and women.'. . . He offered the whisky bottle for the third time. 'No,' I said, 'for I must be getting to the lobsters now.' 'You will drink,' said the old man sharply, and I saw at once that I had offended his peace-offering. I drank a third mouthful. My body glowed like a banked-up fire. 'You will get no lobsters this day,' said the young red-headed fisherman, 'for the storm. You will be the lucky one if you manage to save your creels at all.' I looked round. The delicate egg-shell blue sky was gray as oysters, purple as mussels, and the sun slid through thickening clouds like a wan pearl. 'May God bring us safely through this bad weather and all tempests whatever,' said the old one, 'each one to the safety of his own home.' 'Amen,' spat out the tall vicious one. And at that moment the wind struck us.

All the boats turned for home.

I steered the *Susanna* through rising seas. I felt very brave on account of the Gaelic whisky. I might have been a bit frightened otherwise, for I had never been out in such seas.

I left the lobster creels under the crag and steered straight home. The lobster creels would have to wait until tomorrow, if there were any of them left at all.

The crags gathered round the *Susanna* like ghosts. She lurched and wallowed through the shallower waters. And there, through veils of rain and spindrift, I saw the beach and a solitary woman standing on it. The other boats were in a while ago. The shawled woman stood with the protective hills all round her. The valley offered her to me, Ingi, a figure still as stone. And the savage glad hand of the sea thrust me towards her.

9

Sheepay oatfield was the first to ripen. We went there with our scythes and we cut the oatfield in a day. The field was too steep for the reaper to operate. The women of Sheepay made a supper for us in the evening, as much ale and cheese and bannocks as we could eat. It was very hot in the valley that day. The men worked bare to the waist.

Then Hawkfall barley took the burnish. The field was steep also and right on the top of high crags. Gannets circled under the circling scythes. It was a rather thin crop but it was dark before the last of it was cut. 'The old man of Hawkfall shouldn't have opened that bottle of rum in the middle of the morning,' said Jeremiah of Whalerest, 'and in the hot sun too. It slowed us up....' We had a sleepy supper of oatcakes and ale at Hawkfall.

The good weather held. The third morning the widow of Girss was at every door before daybreak screeching that her oats were ready. We cut her half-acre with the reaper before dinner-time. There was no drink at Girss, neither whisky nor ale, for she was a very religious woman. But she was generous with her bread and slices of mutton. We must have eaten half a sheep. And in the heat her buttermilk tasted better than any beer.

Still the rain kept off. Two-Waters's oats that had been green the day before echoed the sunlight next morning. Peter of Two-Waters, cap in hand, stood in my door. 'We would be pleased,' said the old man, 'if you would help in our field.' 'Get the lobsters to help you,' said I. 'We're sorry for speaking to you as we did that day on the beach,' he said, 'we realize now that you didn't take our lobsters.' 'Keep your mouth shut,' I said, 'and maybe you'll get more harvesters....' I fished all that day alone. The other men turned up at Two-Waters, and after the field was cut they had a great night with fiddles and dancing till after midnight. I couldn't sleep for the noise of them. Ingi said she was sorry I hadn't gone to the Two-Waters oats. 'We must repay hatred with kindness,' she said. 'Anna was very hurt.'

I never saw such sorry-looking agriculture as the barley-field of Cleft, where we all gathered next morning – a few droopy golden beards like kings that had been long in exile. The field wasn't worth to cut. But we cut it. And Andrew of Cleft thanked us. He said if we were thirsty he had a barrel of sweet water at the end of his house. That was the meanest most miserable man in the world. He thanked us very much indeed for our trouble. He only wished he could reward us better, he said (and we all knew for a fact he had a thousand pounds, the legacy from his uncle in Australia, in the bank at Hamnavoe). We left his barley lying like a few slaughtered kings in the high field and we went home. His meanness didn't anger me so much as it might have done because I saw that it was my turn next. My oats had heaved at the sun like a great slow green wave all summer. Now the sun had blessed it. The whole field lay brazen and burnished under a blue sweep of sky. And the wind blessed it continually, sending long murmurs of fulfilment, whispers, secrets, through the thickly congregated stalks. 'Your field tomorrow, Bill,' they all said. I had laid in whisky. Ingi had been brewing and baking for a week (and now her ale for the first time was beginning to taste good). She had boiled eight cock chickens for the harvesters.

The sound of rain and wind woke me after midnight. I could hear the deep gurgle in the throat of the burn. 'Just a shower,' I said to Ingi who had woken also with the noise of rain on the window and the sough in the chimney.

But next morning when I went to the door at first light my cornfield was all squashed and tangled. And the rain still fell, flattening, rotting, burning, destroying. It would have been foolishness trying to cut such mush that day. All the harvesters went out in the storm to save their lobster creels. And the man of Malthouse said it was his turn next for the reaper, 'Because Bill,' he said, 'has missed his turn.'

'It will be a fine day tomorrow,' said Ingi.

The rain lasted a full week.

'The plain truth is,' said Jeremiah of Whalerest, 'you're an unlucky crofter. Some crofters are lucky and some are not. You're a good fisherman, Bill. Stick to the sea.'

10

I spent the whole morning in the office behind Mr Sinclair's general merchant shop in Osmundwall. We had been perhaps a little bit more cordial than the last time we met, but still it was the same as always with Mr Sinclair and me, as if we were closed up together in a hut in the deep Arctic, with no fire in it.

'Well, Bill,' he said, 'if you just sign this paper I think that will be satisfactory to all concerned. I'm a lonely man since Mrs Sinclair died and my chiefest worry now is the happiness of Ingi. You understand that.'

He had proposed before harvest to lend me and Ingi two hundred and fifty pounds at four per cent interest, so that we could finally establish ourselves. In the first instance the loan was to buy more stock and new fishing gear (I had lost all but five of my creels in the October storm).

'Bill,' said Mr Sinclair, 'before you sign that paper I want you to promise me two things. I want you to promise me, for the sake of Ingi, that you won't drink so much. Maybe a small dram on a Saturday night, there's no harm in that, and on a market day, and at New Year of course. And the second thing I want you to promise is this, that you'll go to the services on Sunday. Ingi was brought up in a religious home, and I can tell you this, it hurts her that she has to go to the meeting alone every Sabbath...'

I signed the agreement without bothering to answer him. My two particular saints are Robert Burns and Tom Paine. I was not buying two hundred and fifty pounds worth of hypocrisy.

'William,' cried Mr Sinclair sharply. His assistant hurried in from the shop. 'Witness these signatures, William.' William scratched with the pen at the foot of the paper, then went drooping back to the shop.

'I will deposit the money in Ingi's name in the bank at Hamnavoe,' said Mr Sinclair coldly. 'In Ingi's name. Goodbye.'

I cycled back to the valley, fifteen miles.

When I came between the hills I saw a young woman standing in the door of our house, as if she was keeping guard. It was Anna of Two-Waters, a thick strong ugly girl. Jessie of Topmast was at our peatstack, putting peats in her apron.

I leaned the bicycle against the telegraph pole beside the shop. John Wilson the shopkeeper was standing in his door. When he saw me he popped inside like a rabbit. I knew what it was – I was about to become a father, a tainted unlucky outcast until the christening was over.

I leapt across the burn and walked through the wet field towards the house. Across the valley I saw the widow of Girss, a gray shawl on her head. She was moving slowly towards our house.

Anna looked at me with her young freckled wondering face. 'It's Ingi,' she said. My heart failed and faltered and thudded frighteningly at my ribs. 'The house is full of women,' said Anna. 'Her time has come. It isn't easy for her.'

Just then Williamina of Moorfea came to the door, two empty pails in her hand. 'Is she coming?' Williamina said impatiently to Anna. 'Yes,' said Anna, 'I see her now.' 'I'm just going to the burn for water,' said Williamina. Then she turned to me. 'You go away,' she said. 'You're not needed here today. I think you've done enough.'

The widow of Girss was in the next field now.

Jessie of Topmast came round from my peatstack, her apron full of peats. 'Keep away from here,' she said to me sharply. 'You're not wanted.' Her arms were red with attending to my fire.

By now the widow of Girss was at the corner of the house. Two other women came to the door from inside, Elsie of Calvary and Merrag of Sheepay. They received the midwife reverently and speechlessly, as if she was some kind of priestess. 'You clear off,' Elsie of Calvary whispered harshly at me. 'Get down to your boat. Go somewhere out of here.'

The widow of Girss gave me one cold look before she turned in at the door, followed by the other women except Williamina, who was hurrying across the field to the burn, her empty pails clattering.

Inside, Ingi cried out.

I turned away in a panic. First I made for the shore, thought better of it, and turned to the school-house and my old rationalist teacher Mr Simpson. But the gentle murmur of multiplication tables drifted through the tall window and I knew that the school was still in session. I hurried up the hill to my sheep.

Andrew of Cleft and John of Sheepay saw me coming and veered away from me, each in a different direction. So did the tinker who had been in the hill all month after rabbits.

I was an outcast in my own valley.

Finally the only man I could find to speak to me was Arthur in the ale-house. I remember little of what he said – for an hour it seemed he reeled off the names of the women who to his knowledge had died in childbirth. But his whisky was a comfort. I stayed at the bar counter till it began to get dark. 'It's a pity,' said Arthur, 'Ingi is not a strong woman.'

The lamp was burning in our window when I crossed the field again. 'To hell with them.' I said, 'It's my own house. I'm going in.' I opened the door softly.

Only the high priestess was inside. The servers had all gone home. She turned to me from the bedside, a gentle sorrowful old woman in the lamplight, the widow of Girss. 'Look', she said. Ingi lay asleep in the bed. A small slow pulse beat in her temple. Her damp hair sprawled all over the pillow; one thin bright strand clung to the corner of her fluttering mouth.

The old woman pointed to the wooden cradle that I had made in the seven rainy days of harvest.

'There's your son,' said the widow of Girss.

II

Gales of lamentation I could have put up with from the women, as the terror went through them, the long ritual keening with which they glutted and purified the world from the stain of death. (My grandmother and her neighbours went on for three nights before a funeral, their cries simple and primitive and beautiful as the sea.) Now minister and elders had told them such exhibitions were unseemly and godless; the keening had gradually become in the past twenty years a kind of sickly unction, a litany of the dead person's virtues and sayings and doings – most of them lies – repeated over and over again, a welter of sentimental mush.

The black keening I could have endured.

Ingi lay in the bed, long and pale as a quenched candle. From time to time the child woke up in his cradle and gave a thin cry. Then Anna of Two-Waters would stir and attend to him, while the flat litany went on and on. As for me, I was more of an outcast than ever. None of them paid the slightest attention to me. Once Anna of Two-Waters said, 'Do something. Go and feed the kye. You'll feel better.'

On the third day the missionary came. He opened his bible and the shallow grief of the women became formal, austere, beautiful.

Or ever the silver cord be loosed, or the golden bowl be broken, or the pitcher be broken at the fountain, or the wheel broken at the cistern. Then shall the dust return to earth as it was: and the spirit shall return unto God who gave it.

We buried Ingi that day. Four of us lowered her into her grave – her father, Howie of Two-Waters, Mr Simpson the teacher, myself.

The missionary stood at the graveside and murmured:

All flesh is grass, and the glory of flesh is as the flower thereof. The grass withereth, the flower fadeth, but the word of the Lord shall endure forever.

Afterwards all the men returned from the kirkyard to the house. The women were still there, silent now. 'Give the men whisky,' I said to the widow of Girss, 'and I'll take a cupful myself.' There were two full bottles and a score of cups on the table.

Anna of Two-Waters sat at the fire with the child in her arms. Ever since Ingi's death Anna had fed him and washed him and comforted him. 'Do you want to die as well?' she said to me. 'You haven't eaten for four days. That whisky will finish you.'

'She's in a happier place, poor Ingi,' said Mr Sinclair among the old women. 'That's true,' they cried in their different voices.

'She's in the earth,' I said. 'We've just done putting her there. The ground isn't a particularly happy place to be.'

'She's by with all her troubles,' said Merrag of Sheepay.

The mourners drank the whisky and one by one shook my hand silently and went off home. The missionary stood beside me, dispensing uneasy unction, but I wouldn't speak to him. Mr Sinclair came over to me and said, 'Peter of Two-Waters has spoken to me. As far as I'm concerned it'll be all right. Anna is a hardworking girl. You should think about it....' I didn't know what the man was talking about. 'You'll get your money all right,' I said. 'Go away.'

Anna of Two-Waters put a bowl of hot soup on the table in front of me. 'Eat that,' she said.

The house was getting emptier all the time, as one by one the women made off homeward, their death watch over. At last there were only three of us left, the missionary, Anna of Two-Waters, myself. I heard Mr Sinclair's car coughing distantly among the Coolags.

'Mr McVey the Osmundwall minister has agreed to christen the child on Wednesday next week,' said the missionary.

'He needn't bother,' I said. 'I'm not having any nonsense of that kind.'

Silently the missionary went away.

The child slept, and Anna of Two-Waters rocked the cradle on the stone floor. It was growing dark.

'My father has spoken to me,' she said, 'and so has Mr Sinclair. Finish your soup now.'

'What were they speaking to you about?' I said.

'Somebody must look after this bairn and this house,' said Anna, 'when you're fishing and ploughing. I don't like *you* at all, but I love this bairn of Ingi's. And so I'll do it.'

'Go away,' I said.

'Maybe I'll get used to you after a time,' said Anna.

'Get away out of here, you ugly bitch,' I shouted at her. I took the sleeping baby from the cradle and carried him outside. The first stars shone on him. I carried him down over the fields to the beach. We stood before a slow darkening heave of sea. A fleck of spindrift drifted on to his cheek. The wind had lain in the south-west since before his birth and Ingi's death. He slept on in my arms, with the bitter blessing of the sea on him.

'Be honest,' I said. 'Be against all darkness. Fight on the side of life. Be against ministers, lairds, shopkeepers. Be brave always.'

When I got home Anna was lighting the lamp.

'Put the bairn back in his cradle,' said Anna, 'and then get to bed yourself. You haven't slept for nights. You're a fool.'

She put on her shawl and moved towards the door.

'I'll be back in the morning,' she said.

12

Anna came through the fields from the Christmas service in the school, carrying the shawled child in her arms. I met her at the burn.

'I do believe,' said Anna, 'you've let the fire go out! There's no smoke from the chimney.'

A cold north wind streamed between the Coolags and the Ward over the valley. The stones rang like iron under our feet. Black bags of cloud bursting with snow sat heavily on the hills.

'Everything's settled,' I said to Anna. 'Peter your father has agreed to take over the croft from me. I'm going to concentrate on the fishing. I'll fish for both families, of course. I'm a lucky fisherman. We're to go on living in the house.'

'Yes,' said Anna, 'I think that's the best plan.'

The child was warm enough. His small face lay against

Anna's shoulder with the eyes open and a faint flush on the cheeks.

There were times I could scarcely look into the shifting pool of his face; the skull stared back at me through a thousand trembling resemblances. But today he was a baby like any other baby, a small blind sack of hungers. He began to cry.

'He's tired,' said Anna.

My twenty sheep moved on the hill above the house. In the new year they would belong to old Peter of Two-Waters.

We looked into the byre as we went past. It was warm with the breath of the five kneeling animals. I would have to feed them more hay and turnips before it got darker. The old cow looked round at us with shifting jaws, grave and wondering.

'God help any poor body,' said Anna, 'that has no home on a cold night like this. God help tinkers and all poor wandering folk.'

'Yes,' I said, 'and don't forget the drunkard in the ditch.'

The fire wasn't out after all. There was a deep glow in the heart of the peats. Anna broke the red core with the poker; flames flowered everywhere in the fireplace, and the room was suddenly alive with the rosy shifting dapple.

'It was a beautiful service,' said Anna, 'just lovely. All about Mary and Joseph and the baby and the shepherds and the three kings. I wish you had been there. Who would ever think such things could happen in a byre? Merrag of Sheepay had a new hat on her head. And peedie Tom was so good.'

Before morning, I knew, the valley would be a white blank. And the sea would be flat with the first frost of winter. And, beyond The Kame, fathoms down, the shoals of cod would be moving, bronze soundless streaming legions.

I went out to the shed where I kept my fishing gear.

THE WHALER'S RETURN

FLAWS was at the Arctic whaling all summer and got back to Hamnavoe in the last week of August with seven pounds in gold, and a few shillings, tied in a belt round his middle under his shirt.

He said to Sabiston the harpooner, 'With this money I'm going to rent the croft of Breck and marry Peterina. I'll stay at home from now on. I'll work the three fields and maybe go to the lobsters when it's weather. I'll never see a whale or an iceberg again.'

Sabiston said, 'We'll go into The Arctic Whaler first and wash the salt out of our throats.'

In The Arctic Whaler they sat on barrels and drank ale. Then some other whaling men came in. They were all glad to be home. A few of them began to spend freely, buying rounds of rum for everyone in the bar. When it came to Flaws's turn, he bought rum for everyone too. Then, alarmed at his extravagance – he had fractured one of his sovereigns to buy the round of rum and the loose copper and silver lay in his hand like so much cold mud and snow – he rose to his feet and said to Sabiston, 'Now I'm going to walk home to Birsay.'

Before he went, Phimister of the *Skua* sang 'The Harray Crab'. The north-west men roared out the chorus.

Phimister sang the song well. Everyone crowded about him with drink, Flaws also.

Flaws hoisted his box on his shoulder. He left The Arctic Whaler at ten in the morning and set out for Birsay. At the north end of Hamnavoe he saw that there was a new ale-house called The White Horse. It must have opened for the first time during the summer.

He put his head through the door and saw a few farmers sitting round the fire drinking. The barmaid was standing at a mirror twisting her yellow hair at the back of her head. At last she got a fine burnished knot on it and drove a pin through to hold it in place.

Flaws hadn't seen a woman for six months. He went in and asked for a mug of ale.

'We only sell whisky here,' said the girl, 'threepence a glass.'

'A glass of whisky then,' said Flaws.

He thought it might be the last chance he would ever have to speak to a pretty girl. Peterina was good and hard-working, but rather ugly.

Flaws stood at the bar and drank his whisky. The four farmers sat round the fire saying little. It was Wednesday in Hamnavoe, the day they drove in their beasts to sell at the Mart.

'Do you do much trade in The White Horse?' said Flaws to the barmaid.

'We welcome only the better sort of person here,' said the girl, 'the quiet country men, not the ruffians and tramps from the herring boats and the whalers. And of course the office workers too, and business people. We're always very busy in the evening after the shops and offices close. No fighting scum from the boats ever cross the threshold of The White Horse.' Out of her pretty mouth she spat on the stone floor.

Flaws was glad he was wearing his decent suit of broadcloth, the one his old mother always packed in mothballs at the bottom of his chest for departures and home-comings.

He ordered two glasses of whisky, one for the barmaid. She smiled at him sweetly. They touched rims till the glasses made a small music and the whisky trembled into yellow circles. Flaws was transported. He longed to touch her burnished head. Given time, solitude, and another dram or two, he could well imagine himself kissing her across the bar.

'I haven't seen you in The White Horse before,' said the barmaid. 'What is your occupation, sir?'

'God forgive me for telling a lie,' said Flaws to himself. Then he squared his shoulders and said, 'I only visit the islands now and then. I'm a commercial traveller. I travel for earthenware and china.'

The barmaid glittered at him with eyes, teeth, hair, rings.

The door opened and Small the lawyer's clerk tiptoed in, his drunken nose (Flaws thought) redder than ever. He went up to the bar slowly, eyeing Flaws the way a hunter eyes his quarry. 'If it isn't Flaws!' he cried at last. 'If it isn't my old friend! And did you catch many whales at Greenland, eh? I can smell the blubber and the oil with you. I warrant you have a fine pile of sovereigns in your pocket. You're the first seaman ever to get into The White Horse.'

Flaws could have killed the little drunken clerk at that moment. The barmaid was suddenly looking at him with eyes as cold as stones.

Flaws hoisted his box on his shoulder and made for the door without a word. His pocket was heavy with more silver and copper; he had broken another sovereign in The White Horse. He stood, hot with shame and resentment, on the road outside.

'A commercial traveller!' cried Small the lawyer's clerk at the bar. Suddenly the interior of The White Horse was loud with merriment, the deep bass laughter of the farmers mingling with the falsetto mirth of the lawyer's clerk and the merry tinkle of the barmaid.

Flaws walked on towards Birsay, red in the face.

'Thank God to be clear of Hamnavoe at least', said Flaws to himself. There were forty pubs and ale-houses in the one long twisting street of the town. A good many of the returned whalers would have visited them all by the week-end. By Monday morning Sabiston and a few others wouldn't have a sixpence left. Flaws considered that he had done well, only drinking in two howffs.

It was a long road, sixteen miles, to Birsay. The day was fine, with a clear cold sky. Oats were ripening in a field at the end of the town. The rum and whisky put a rhythm in his step. How grand it was to be walking on the firm roads of home once more, not lurching about on the frozen deck of a whaling ship, with death everywhere round you, in berg and whale and unquiet water, and worst of all in the sudden knives of the drunk dice-players at midnight. Flaws had had nothing to do with them. His bible had kept him safe. He had read a chapter every night in his hammock before turning over to sleep, while the little ivory cubes rattled wickedly on the lid of a sea chest.

In Sandwick Flaws began to feel hungry.

An old woman called Bella Jean Bews kept a lodging house at Yesnaby, half a mile off the road. Flaws thought he might get a plate of salt fish there, enough to keep him going.

A rich smell met him in the door. Bella Jean Bews had been both baking and brewing. A tall pile of new bannocks smoked on her table, and a kirn beside the fire seethed with ale.

'Yes,' said Bella Jean Bews, 'come in, boy. I'll give thee something to eat.' She put two boiled crabs in front of him on the bare table and a thick hot buttered bannock. 'Help theeself,' she said.

Flaws ate till there was a comfortable tightness across his stomach. 'Have you such a thing as a drop of milk?' said Flaws.

'Better than milk,' said Bella Jean Bews. She dipped a wooden bowl in the kirn and brought it, brimming with green ale, to Flaws. 'Drink that, boy,' she said, 'that'll help thee on thee way. Are thu gang far?'

'To Birsay,' said Flaws, and tasted some of the ale. It was a raw sweet unfinished brew.

'A fair walk,' said Bella Jean Bews. 'Drink up, boy.'

Suddenly she leaned forward and put her face close to his. 'Is thee name Flaws?' she said.

'It is,' said Flaws.

'And thu've been at the Davis Strait since April,' she said, 'at the whales?'

'Yes,' said Flaws.

'And thu're contracted to be married at harvest to Peterina Gold of Fadoon?'

'That's a fact,' said Flaws.

'Well,' said Bella Jean Bews, 'I'm glad to see thee. Peterina's father, old Jock Gold the roadman, was kicked on the head with a horse the week after midsummer. He lay down in the ditch with the red hoof mark on him. The peat-cutters from the hill found him there. They took him home to Fadoon in a cart. Peterina said nothing when they carried her father into the house. She didn't even have a drink of whisky to give to the peat-cutters. It's a poor house thu're marrying into. Peterina put a shawl over her head and she walked over the hills here to Yesnaby. The two of us made for Birsay at once to get there before it was dark. There was Jock Gold on the floor, with a red wound the shape of a horse-shoe on his skull. Peterina took a long gray shirt from the chest under the bed, Jock's shroud that his mother had sewed for him as soon as he was a grown man, for nobody can tell when death will come. Then I washed the body and I put the gray shirt on it and I folded his hands. We lit the lamp then – it was dark by this time. Peterina wrote in the big bible in the window, "John Gold, killed by a horse the week after midsummer." There was little in the cupboard, some oatmeal and a sup of milk. It's a poor woman thu'll get for a wife. Peterina never shed one tear for her father. "He was a queer bitter man," she said. "The house'll be sweeter without him."...Later, near midnight, she turned to me and she said, "I have no money to pay you for your services this night. Forgive me. But Andrew Flaws will pay you when he gets back from the whales, if he ever gets back, for we see how dangerous life is, even for a roadman."...I stayed with her all that night. On my way home, at first light next morning, I knocked at the gravedigger's door.'

'God save him,' said Flaws.

'Amen,' said Bella Jean Bews. 'Drink up. There's plenty of ale. I have another crab in the pot.'

'Just a mug of ale,' said Flaws. 'He was a queer twisted bitter man. Peterina has had a poor life with him this seven years past.'

'That's in God's hands,' said Bella Jean Bews. 'Don't drink so fast. It's very strong ale. My fee for the shrouding is half a guinea.'

Flaws took a sovereign out of his belt and laid it on the table.

'There,' he said. 'I want no change.'

'For your wedding,' said Bella Jean Bews, 'you'll be wanting a serving-woman. And soon after that, no doubt, you'll be needing a midwife for Peterina. I'll be glad to come.'

'Yes,' said Flaws. 'Give me a last mug of strong ale, then I'll go.'

Flaws walked on through the parish of Sandwick, his feet easy on the road, the box on his shoulder as light as if it was stuffed with larks' feathers. Some of the oat-fields he passed were still green, others were touched with the first gold. They whispered densely round him in the stillness; the countryside was one huge conspiracy for the benefit of bewintered man. Then, in a freshet of wind, deep surges went through the oatfields, and the barley undulated and shimmered like new silk. It would be a good harvest. He hurried on; next year he himself, the new crofter of Breck, would take part in this ritual of the corn, the cycle of birth, love, death, resurrection. He hurried on. An awkward old man had died up at Fadoon. Soon Peterina would write in the black bible, 'Andrew Flaws and Peterina Gold, married at the end of harvest', and afterwards, in a weak hand, 'Andrew John Gold Flaws, first son to Andrew and Peterina Flaws, born in the time of hay.'. . . So life went on. The seed was buried, the ripe corn fell, bread was broken.

He hurried along the road to Birsay. There were six ale-houses between Sandwick and Birsay. Flaws decided that he would visit none of them. The only person he wanted to see now was Peterina. He hurried on past Scarth's ale-house and Wylie's ale-house (though there was a sound of bag-pipes from there) and Spence's ale-house.

At the gate of Halcro's ale-house, as he was hurrying past, a hand shot out of the bushes and gripped Flaws by the arm. He almost dropped his sea-chest with shock. A grizzled sly laughing face was stuck into his. It was Halcro himself, the landlord.

'Andrew Flaws,' he cried. 'Welcome home, Andrew Flaws. I'm glad to see thee, Andrew Flaws. What's all this hurry, Andrew Flaws? Andrew Flaws, thu must have a drink with me.'

'No', said Flaws, still in a trance of love and labour and fulfilment. 'No.'

'What kind of a way is that to speak, Andrew Flaws?' said Halcro. 'Come on in. The whales are all dead and men must live and rejoice.'

'No,' said Flaws.

Halcro dragged him by the arm towards the ale-house. 'Men,' he yelled to the drinkers inside, 'look who's here, Andrew Flaws. Andrew Flaws is home again. He's wanting to celebrate, Andrew Flaws.'

Flaws struggled like a fly in honey.

Suddenly the door of Halcro's ale-house was crammed with faces and pewter mugs.

'Andrew Flaws!' they all cried, and there was a tilting of heads and a steeper tilting of mugs and a working of throats. 'Welcome home, Andrew Flaws,' said a score of frothy beards.

So there was no escape for Flaws at Halcro's. He drank with the Sandwick men till the ale-house plunged and swayed like a Lofoten whaler in a gale. Pewter clashed and foamed round him. He was clapped on the shoulder a hundred times.

'A drink for Andrew Flaws,' cried old Halcro.

Flaws took a sovereign out of his belt to repay their hospitality. The sovereign was quickly broken up, first into florins, then into sixpences, then into pennies, and all the fragments flowed back into Halcro's till.

Soon the ale ran out and they all began to drink Norwegian spirits, aquavit.

Late in the afternoon Flaws said seriously to Peter of Skaill who was standing beside him, 'Now I don't feel as if I was on a whaling boat, it's more as if I was in the belly of a whale, wound in guts. Peter, I must go.'

He made a great lurch between the barrel and the door.

The noise of the ale-house faded.

He found himself on the road again, alone, a bewildered Jonah.

'What I want to know, sir, is this,' said Flaws. 'Was he properly buried?'

'No question of it,' said Mr Selly the minister. 'I performed the ceremony myself. I said a prayer in the house and another prayer at the graveside. Also I read an appropriate passage from holy writ, *Man goeth to his long home*. Death is a great mystery. There is, though, Andrew, one small matter, the funeral was conducted with maimèd rites, as Hamlet described it. Neither the minister's fee nor the gravedigger's fee was paid. Well, of course, we must expect such omissions from time to time. In this case the girl is poor. The omissions can always be repaired when circumstances improve.'

'How much do the fees come to?' said Flaws.

'Five shillings,' said Mr Selly, 'a half-crown for the gravedigger and the same amount for me.'

Flaws brought a handful of silver and copper out of his pocket. He picked out a large crown piece and set it on the manse table. 'There,' he said.

'Splendid,' said Mr Selly. He unlocked a metal box on the sideboard and put the crown piece inside. 'If they were all like you, Andrew.'

'How much is a wedding fee?' said Flaws.

'Half-a-crown,' said Mr Selly.

Flaws picked a half-crown out of the heaped treasure in his fist and laid it on the table. 'I'll be marrying Peterina Gold of Fadoon at the end of harvest,' he said.

'Very good,' said Mr Selly. 'I'm glad to hear it. You will have to see the Session Clerk, of course, Mr Work, so that the banns can be read in church. Splendid.' He rattled the half-crown into the cash box and locked it. 'I think we can dispense with receipts. We trust each other, don't we? Andrew, I think this calls for a little celebration.' He opened the cupboard door and took out a bottle and two glasses.

Flaws said, 'I want to get to Fadoon before it's dark.'

'Of course,' said Mr Selly. 'I understand. But this, Andrew, is the very best brandy, cognac. Andrew, I know you will tell nobody about this, but there was a French ship in the bay one night last month in the dark of the moon. Twenty-one kegs of brandy were taken off her, unbeknown to the excise, plus a huge quantity of tobacco. Twenty-one kegs. Through an agency that I shall not divulge, one of those kegs found its way to the Manse.' He winked at Flaws, then carefully filled two glasses with the brandy.

'Andrew,' he said, raising his glass, 'may your marriage be long and prosperous. Peterina is a good girl, and poverty is no crime.'

'Thank you,' said Flaws, and gulped the foreign stuff down. Tears stood in his eyes. He got to his feet. 'Goodnight, minister.'

'Goodnight, Andrew,' said Mr Selly. 'It's a good spirit, isn't it? I'm glad you're home again. Mr Partridge-Simpson the laird is keeping the croft of Breck for you. I spoke to him one day last week. We'll be seeing you in your pew on Sunday as usual? I hope so.'

In the flagstone quarry a mile past the Manse the tinkers

were holding some kind of celebration. A large fire was burning, and round it the tinkers sat in groups. From time to time one of them gave vent to a wild cry, then there was silence again. A young girl went round with a jug, pouring drink into their cups.

It was dark on the road. Flaws felt very tired, as if he had walked a hundred miles since morning, as if he had made a wide detour round the real world and was now wandering deeper and deeper into the heart of fantasy.

He left the road and crouched among the bushes in the darkness, watching the tinkers' ritual.

It was a wedding.

Will and Mary sat at opposite ends of a large flat stone that had been hewn out of the quarry a long time ago. They were in their usual rags, except that clean white handkerchiefs were tied round their throats. Between them sat Ezra, the chief of the clan, as solemn as a king or a priest. Tonight he was the celebrant at the mysteries.

An old woman, Heather, stood in front of them, a little to one side, her voice rising every now and again in a passion of denunciation.

The other tinkers sat well behind, in dark intent groups. The only moving figure was the girl who carried round the jug of spirits.

'You, Will,' cried Heather, 'stole three hens from the farm of the Glebe in April and in the month of June you took a sack of peats from Mucklehouse and you took a tin of syrup from the grocer's van in Dounby on the Thursday of the Agricultural Show. Didn't you poach salmon out of the burn at Strathnaver in Sutherlandshire? You did. And you are nowise fit to be the husband of this good girl, Mary.'

'Answer, Will,' said Ezra.

'Things happen,' said Will, 'both good and evil. I will keep bread in Mary's mouth.'

'I take him for my man,' said Mary.

'It is well spoken,' said Ezra.

Everybody drank out of their cups, except Will, Mary, and the old woman, the devil's advocate.

Flaws peered through the screen of branches. He felt a tap on his shoulder. The dark girl, the cup-bearer, stood beside him, holding out a mug with liquor in it. She smiled at him, then softly returned to the barrel to refill her jug. Flaws took a deep drink. His mouth and throat were so scoured with rum, whisky, ale, aquavit, and brandy that this stuff went down as tasteless as water; but he felt a slow dark smoulder in his stomach.

The old woman suddenly screamed out, 'Will, didn't you get drunk at the Kirkwall Market and fight with a Norwegian sailor in the Laverock, and didn't they keep you in jail all that week-end? Didn't you get drunk at the Harvest Home in Canisby, Caithness, and break the fiddle over Gunn the fiddler's head because Gunn was playing the reel wrong? Weren't you drunk three times between the Hamnavoe Market and Hallowe'en, and again four times between Hallowe'en and Hogmanay? And you shall not be the husband of this good girl, Mary.'

'Answer,' said Ezra.

'Things happen,' said Will, 'both good and bad. I will keep a shawl about her shoulders.'

'And I take him for my man,' said Mary.

'It is well spoken,' said Ezra.

The tinkers drank, all except Will, Mary, and old Heather. The girl was beside Flaws once more. The spirit went into his cup, a tiny sweet music. Then she was off like a shadow.

The old woman began again, beating the air with her fist. 'Will,' she cried, 'what were you after the age of fourteen? Not a virgin. You tore the buttons off Liz's dress and you laid Dolina down in a wet ditch and you went naked at midnight into Belle's tent the time her man Sam was away at the rag gathering. The girl Seena in Dounby has a bairn the

74

very spit of you. You kissed the laird's servant lass at the end
of the stable door – the mark of the factor's whip is still on
your throat from that on-carry. You must not be the husband
of this good girl Mary.'

Heather's shrieks echoed from wall to wall of the quarry.

'Answer,' said Ezra.

'Things happen,' said Will, 'both good and bad. I will light
fires for her in winter.'

'And I take him for my man,' said Mary.

'It is well spoken,' said Ezra.

The tinkers raised their mugs. The dark girl poked the fire
and a flame roared high. Then she slipped behind the bush
with her jug and filled Flaws's cup. This time she did not
look at him.

Old Heather began to speak again, but now in a gentle
voice. 'You, Mary. I will speak against you. With most brides
it's no trouble to say a lot, with their whoring and garbing
and gossiping. But there's little against you, Mary. You lost
a bag of pins, a shillingsworth, at the Dounby Market the year
before last. You scorched a rabbit once that was stewing over
the fire. The solder came off a tin pail you made for the Holm
doctor. So you will not be the wife of this good man Will.'

'Answer,' said Ezra.

'Things happen, both good and bad,' said Mary. 'I will
carry his children proudly.'

'I take her for my wife,' said Will.

'It is well spoken,' said Ezra.

The tinkers rose to their feet, drank, cheered, and threw
the dregs of their whisky into the fire. Then they all sat down
again.

Quickly the girl filled up every cup in the quarry. This time
she did not carry her jug over to Flaws. She stooped and
whispered in the ear of Angus, a young powerful tinker, and
pointed to the bush where the intruder squatted unseen.

'Now,' said Ezra, 'the bucket.'

Old Heather placed a tin pail between the fire and the ceremonial stone. Will rose from his place and went over to the pail. He loosed his breeches and urinated into it. Then it was Mary's turn. She hoisted up her skirt, squatted over the pail, and urinated into it. Solemnly Ezra lifted the pail and swilled it seven times in sunward circles. 'Whoever can separate this water,' he cried, 'can separate this man Will and this woman Mary.' Then he emptied out the mingled urine on the quarry floor.

Will and Mary kissed each other.

The tinkers danced, yelled, shouted, rose to their feet. A fiddle began to play. Dancing broke out all over the quarry. A dog in a nearby farm barked. Ezra and old Heather circled each other, slow and grave. The ritual bearing round of drink was forgotten; now the tinkers held their mouths under the dripping tap of the barrel and staggered away. The feet beat on and the dance grew wilder. Where was the beautiful cup-bearer? Flaws wanted to dance with her. He wanted to hear the sound of her voice. He wanted to ask her why she had bypassed him on her last circuit and why she had whispered so secretly to Angus. He wanted to kiss her before he gave his kisses to Peterina for ever. He rose from the heart of the bush and wandered uncertainly towards the flames and the din. There she was, putting a sea-bleached board into the fire, her bare arm rosy in the flame. He made for her. The fiddle screamed in his ear. Ezra passed his reeking pipe to Heather. 'Girl,' said Flaws. She turned a blank cold face on him.

A hand clawed and tore.

Then the black snarling wave was all about him.

He woke in a ditch below Fadoon, in broad daylight, a mile and more from the tinkers' quarry.

Painfully he got to his feet. His bones creaked. Water ran out of his sleeve. His tongue lay in his mouth like a filthy rag.

His first thought was for his money. His fingers groped

under his shirt. There were two sovereigns left in his belt. Out of his pocket he brought twelve shillings in silver and a few coppers. A surge of relief went through him. He would at least be able to pay the first half year's rent for Breck, two guineas.

He walked between two fields to Fadoon. The last green was gone from the oats now; the harvest burnish was on every blade. There was a curl of smoke from the roof and the door stood open. He bowed his head under the lintel and went in. Peterina was sitting at her spinning wheel.

'Peace to this place,' said Flaws.

'You're back from the whales, Andrew Flaws', said Peterina.

'Yes,' he said.

'You're in better shape than I expected,' said Peterina. 'There are thirty-four ale-houses in the town of Hamnavoe and sixteen ale-houses on the road between Hamnavoe and Birsay. Some men from the ships are a long time getting home.'

'I have the rent for the croft of Breck,' said Flaws, 'and a shilling or two besides.'

'We move in in November,' said Peterina. She went over to the cupboard and brought out a jug and a bannock. 'Bring over your chair to the table,' she said. 'Here's some bread and ale.'

While Flaws was eating, Peterina said, 'There's little news in the parish. My father was killed by a horse in the month of June. God forgive me for speaking ill of the dead, but it's been a quiet house since then. A quiet house but a bare house. I've had to live on the parochial poor fund since the funeral. With the shame of that, I don't show my face in the public. I wasn't able to pay any of the death money, neither the shrouding fee nor the fee for the digging of the grave nor the minister's fee.'

'I saw to all that on my way home,' said Flaws. 'Everything is paid.'

'That was a good thing you did, Andrew Flaws,' said Peterina.

'And the wedding fee is paid too,' said Flaws.

'That will be in the last week of September,' said Peterina. 'I will try to be a good wife to you, Andrew Flaws. Before that time I must make a blanket for the bed, and a christening shawl for the first bairn, and two shrouds, one for you and one for me, for no man can tell the day or the hour, and we must be ready at all times.' The wheel went round and the new gray wool slid between her fingers.

'I tarred the boat down at the beach,' said Peterina. 'You'll fish until such time as we reap our first harvest at Breck.'

'Yes,' said Flaws.

'There was a wedding last night at the tinkers' camp in the quarry,' said Peterina. 'It was a wild celebration. I heard fiddles at three o'clock in the morning.'

'Yes,' said Flaws. He drank the last of the ale. It was the sweetest drink he had ever tasted. 'I think I'll sleep for an hour or two,' he said, 'then I'll maybe catch a few haddocks, before sunset. The laird will be wanting harvesters tomorrow or the day after.'

TARTAN

THEY anchored the *Eagle* off the rock, in shallow water, between the horns of a white sandy bay. It was a windy morning. Behind the bay stretched a valley of fertile farms.

'We will visit those houses,' said Arnor the helmsman. Olaf who was the skipper that voyage said he would bide on the ship. He had a poem to make about rounding Cape Wrath that would keep him busy.

Four of the Vikings – Arnor, Havard, Kol, Sven – waded ashore. They carried axes in their belts.

Gulls rose from the crag, circled, leaned away to the west.

The first house they came to was empty. But the door stood open. There was a shirt drying on the grass and a dog ran round them in wild noisy circles. Two sheep were tethered near the back wall.

'We will take the sheep as we return,' said Havard.

Between this house and the next house was a small burn running fast and turbid after the recent rain. One by one they leapt across it. Kol did not quite make the far bank and got his feet wet. 'No doubt somebody will pay for this,' he said.

'That was an unlucky thing to happen,' said Sven. 'Everything Kol has done this voyage has been wrong.'

Another dog came at them silently from behind, a tooth grazed Arnor's thigh. Arnor's axe bit the dog to the backbone. The animal howled twice and died where he lay.

In the second house they found a fire burning and a pot of broth hanging over it by a hook. 'This smell makes my nostrils twitch,' said Sven. 'I am sick of the salted beef and raw fish that we eat on board the *Eagle*.'

They sat round the table and put the pot of soup in the centre. While they were supping it Sven raised his head and saw a girl with black hair and black eyes looking at them from the open door. He got to his feet, but by the time he reached the door the girl was three fields away.

They finished the pot of broth. 'I burnt my mouth,' said Kol.

There were some fine woollen blankets in a chest under the bed. 'Set them out,' said Arnor, 'they'll keep us warm at night on the sea.'

'They are not drinking people in this valley,' said Havard, who was turning everything upside down looking for ale.

They crossed a field to the third house, a hovel. From the door they heard muttering and sighing inside. 'There's breath in this house,' said Kol. He leapt into the middle of the floor with a loud berserk yell, but it might have been a fly buzzing in the window for all the attention the old woman paid to him. 'Ah,' she was singing over the sheeted dead child on the bed, 'I thought to see you a shepherd on Morven, or maybe a fisherman poaching salmon at the mouth of the Naver. Or maybe you would be a man with lucky acres and the people would come from far and near to buy your corn. Or you might have been a holy priest at the seven altars of the west.'

There was a candle burning at the child's head and a cross lay on his breast, tangled in his cold fingers.

Arnor, Havard, and Sven crossed themselves in the door. Kol slunk out like an old dog.

They took nothing from that house but trudged uphill to a neat gray house built into the sheer brae.

At the cairn across the valley, a mile away, a group of plaided men stood watching them.

At the fourth door a voice called to them to come in. A thin man was standing beside a loom with a half-made web in it. 'Strangers from the sea,' he said, 'you are welcome. You have the salt in your throats and I ask you to accept ale from Malcolm the weaver.'

They stood round the door and Malcolm the weaver poured horns of ale for each of them.

'This is passable ale,' said Havard. 'If it had been sour, Malcolm the weaver, we would have stretched you alive on your loom. We would have woven the thread of eternity through you.'

Malcolm the weaver laughed.

'What is the name of this place?' said Arnor.

'It is called Durness,' said Malcolm the weaver. 'They are good people here, except for the man who lives in the tall house beyond the cairn. His name is Duncan, and he will not pay me for the cloth I wove for him last winter, so that he and his wife and his snovelly-nosed children could have coats when the snow came.'

'On account of the average quality of your ale, we will settle matters with this Duncan,' said Arnor. 'Now we need our cups filled again.'

They stayed at Malcolm the weaver's house for an hour and more, and when they got up to go Kol staggered against the door. 'Doubtless somebody will pay for this,' he said thickly.

They took with them a web of cloth without asking leave of Malcolm. It was a gray cloth of fine quality and it had a thick green stripe and a thin brown stripe running up and down and a very thick black stripe cutting across it horizontally. It was the kind of Celtic weave they call tartan.

'Take it, take it by all means,' said Malcolm the weaver.

'We were going to take it in any case,' said Sven.

'Tell us,' said Havard from the door, 'who is the girl in Durness with black hair and black eyes and a cleft chin?'

'Her name is Morag,' said Malcolm the weaver, 'and she is the wife of John the shepherd. John has been on the hill all week with the new lambs. I think she is lonely.'

'She makes good soup,' said Arnor. 'And if I could get hold of her for an hour I would cure her loneliness.'

It took them some time to get to the house of Duncan because they had to support Kol who was drunk. Finally they stretched him out along the lee wall of the house. 'A great many people will suffer,' said Kol, and began to snore.

The Gaelic men were still standing beside the cairn, a good distance off, and now the girl with black hair had joined them. They watched the three Vikings going in at the fifth door.

In Duncan's house were three half-grown children, two boys and a girl. 'Where is the purchaser of coats?' said Havard. 'Where is the ruination of poor weavers? Where is Duncan your father?'

'When the Viking ship came into the bay,' said a boy with fair hair, the oldest of the children, 'he took the mare from the stable and put our mother behind him on the mare's back and rode off south to visit his cousin Donald in Lairg.'

'What will you three do when we burn this house down?' said Arnor.

'We will stand outside,' said the boy, 'and we will be warm first and afterwards we will be cold.'

'And when we take away the coats for which Malcolm the weaver has not been paid?' said Arnor.

'Then we will be colder than ever,' said the boy.

'It is a clever child,' said Sven, 'that will doubtless utter much wisdom in the councils of Caithness in a few years' time. Such an orator should not go cold in his youth.'

They gave the children a silver Byzantine coin from their crusade the previous summer and left the house.

They found Kol where they had left him, at the wall, but he was dead. Someone had cut his throat with a corn-hook.

'Now we should destroy the valley,' said Havard.

'No,' said Arnor, 'for I'm heavy with the weaver's drink and it's getting dark and I don't want sickles in my beard. And besides all that the world is well rid of a fool.'

They walked down to the house where the sheep were tethered. Now eight dark figures, including Malcolm the weaver and Morag and the clever-tongued boy (Duncan's son), followed them all the way, keeping to the other side of the ridge. The men were armed with knives and sickles and hayforks. The moon was beginning to rise over the Caithness hills.

They killed the two sheep and carried them down the beach on their backs. The full moon was opening and shutting on the sea like the Chinese silk-and-ivory fan that Sven had brought home from Byzantium.

They had a good deal of trouble getting those awkward burdens of wool and mutton on board the *Eagle*.

'Where is Kol?' said Olaf the skipper.

'In a ditch with his throat cut,' said Sven. 'He was fortunate in that he died drunk.'

The Durness people stood silent on the beach, a score of them, and the old bereaved woman raised her hand against them in silent malediction.

The sail fluttered and the blades dipped and rose through lucent musical rings.

'The poem has two good lines out of seven,' said Olaf. 'I will work on it when I get home to Rousay.'

He steered the *Eagle* into the Pentland Firth.

Off Stroma he said, 'The tartan will go to Ingerd in Westray. Kol kept her a tattered trull all her days, but with this cloth she will be a stylish widow for a winter or two.'

TITHONUS

FRAGMENTS FROM THE DIARY OF A LAIRD

THEY are all, especially the women, excited in Torsay today. There is a new child in the village, a little girl. The birth has happened in a house where – so Traill the postman assured me – no one for the past ten years has expected it. The door of Maurice Garth the fisherman and his wife Armingert had seemed to be marked with the sign of barrenness. They were married twenty-one years ago, when Maurice was thirty and Armingert nineteen. One might have expected a large family, five or six at least, from such a healthy devoted pair. (They had both come from tumultuous households to the cold empty cottage at the end of the village.) But the years passed and no young voice broke the quiet dialogue of Maurice and Armingert. To all the islanders it seemed a pity: nothing but beautiful children could have come from their loins.

I was hauling my dinghy up the loch shore this afternoon – it was too bright a day, the trout saw through every gesture and feint – when I saw the woman on the road above. It seemed to me then that she had been waiting to speak to me for some time. I knew who she must be as soon as she opened her mouth. The butterings of her tongue, and the sudden knife flashes, had been described to me often enough. She was Maggie Swintoun. I had been well warned about her by the factor and the minister and the postman. Her idle and wayward tongue, they told me, had done harm to the reputation of more than one person in Torsay; so I'm sure that when I turned my loch-dazzled face to her it did not wear a welcoming expression.

'O sir, you'll never guess,' she said, in the rapt secret voice of all news bearers. 'A bairn was born in the village this morning, and at the Garth cottage of all places – a girl. I think it's right that you should know. Dr Wayne from Hamnavoe took it into the world. I was there helping. I could hardly believe it when they sent for me.'

The face was withdrawn from the loch side. A rare morning was in front of her, telling the news in shop, smithy, manse and at the doors of all the crofts round about.

I mounted my horse that, patient beast, had been cropping the thin loch-side grass all morning and cantered back to The Hall over the stony dusty road.

Now I knew why a light had been burning at two o'clock in the cottage at the end of the village. I had got up at that time to let Tobias the cat in.

This is the first child to be born in the island since I came to be laird here. I feel that in some way she belongs to me. I stood at the high window of The Hall looking down at the Garth cottage till the light began to fade.

The generations have been renewed. The island is greatly enriched since yesterday.

I suppose that emotionally I am a kind of neutral person, in the sense that I attract neither very much love nor very much dislike. It is eight years since I arrived from London to live in the island that my grand-uncle, the laird of Torsay, a man I had never seen in my life, left to me. On the slope behind the village with its pier and shop and church is The Hall – the laird's residence – that was built in the late seventeenth century, a large elegant house with eighteen rooms, and a garden, and a stable. I am on speaking terms with everyone in the village and with most of the farmers and crofters in the hinterland. Certain people – William Copinsay the shopkeeper, Maggie Swintoun, Grossiter from the farm of Wear – I pass with as curt a nod as I can manage. If I do have a friend, I suppose he must be James MacIntosh who came to be the schoolmaster in the village two summers ago. We play chess in the school-house every Friday night, summer and winter. Occasionally, when he is out walking with his dog, he calls at my place and we drink whatever is in the whisky decanter. (But I insist that his dog, a furtive collie called Joe who occasionally bares his teeth at passers-by, is not let further than the kitchen – Tobias must not be annoyed.) MacIntosh comes from Perth. He is a pleasant enough man. I think his chief interest is politics, but I do nothing to encourage him when he starts about the Irish question, or the Liberal schism, or the suffragettes, or what the Japanese can be expected to do in such and such an eventuality. I am sure, if I let him go on, that some fine evening he will declare himself to be a socialist. I set the decanter squarely between us whenever I hear the first opinionated murmurings; in those malty depths, and there alone, will any argument be.

I think MacIntosh is quite happy living in this island. He is too lazy and too good-natured to be hustled about in a big city school. It is almost certain that he has no real vocation for his job. He has gone to the university, and taken an arts degree, and then enrolled in teaching for want of anything better. But perhaps I do him wrong; perhaps he is dedicated after all to make 'clever de'ils' of the Torsay children. At any rate, the parents and the minister – our education committee representative – seem to have no objection to him. My reason for thinking that he is without taste or talent for the classroom is that he never mentions his work to me; but there again it could simply be, as with politics, that he receives no encouragement.

There is a curious shifting relationship between us, sometimes cordial, sometimes veiled and hostile. He becomes aware from time to time of the social gulf between us, and it is on these occasions that he says and does things to humble me – I must learn that we are living now in the age of equality. But under it all he is such a good-natured chap; after ten minutes or so of unbated tongues we are at peace again over chess-board or decanter.

Last night MacIntosh said, between two bouts of chess in the school-house, 'It's a very strange thing, I did not think I could ever be so intrigued by a child. Most of them are formed of the common clay after all. O, you know what I mean – from time to time a beautiful child, or a clever child, comes to the school, and you teach him or her for a year or two, then away they go to the big school in the town, or back to work on the farm, and you never think more about them. But this pupil is just that wee bit different.'

'What on earth are you talking about?' I said.

'The Garth girl who lives at the end of the village – Thora – you know, her father has the fishing boat *Rain Goose*.'

'Is that her name, Thora?' I said. (For I had seen the quiet face among a drift of school-children in the playground, at four o'clock, going home then alone to Maurice and Armingert's door. I had seen bright hair at the end of the small stone pier, waiting for a boat to come in from the west. I had seen the solemn clasped hands, bearing the small bible, outside the kirk door on a Sunday morning. But beyond that the girl and I had never exchanged a single word. As I say, I did not even know her name till last night.)

'She is a very strange girl, that one,' said MacIntosh. 'There is a *something* about her. Would you please not drop your ash on the mat? (There's an ash tray.) I'm not like some folk. I can't afford to buy a new mat every month. Mrs Baillie asked me to mention it to you.'

My pipe and his dog cancel each other out. Mrs Baillie is his housekeeper.

'To me she looks an ordinary enough child,' I said. 'In what way is she different?'

MacIntosh could not say how this girl was different. She was made of the common clay – 'like all of us, like all of us,' he hastened to assure me, thereby putting all the islanders, including the laird and Halcro the beachcomber, on the same footing. Still, there was something special about the girl, he insisted, goodness knows what. . . .

MacIntosh won the third hard-fought game. He exulted. Victory always makes him reckless and generous. 'Smoke, man, smoke in here any time you like. To hell with Mrs Baillie. Get your pipe out. I'll sweep any ash up myself.'

I met Thora Garth on the brae outside the kirk as I was going home from the school-house. She put on me a brief pellucid unsmiling look as we passed. She was carrying a pail of milk from the farm of Gardyke.

Fifteen years ago, in my grand-uncle's day, the island women stopped and curtsied whenever the laird went past. A century ago a single glance from the great man of The Hall turned them to stone in their fields.

All that is changed.

Traill the postman had put a letter through my window while I was at the school-house. The familiar official writing was on the envelope. I lit the lamp. I was secure in my island for another six months. The usual hundred pounds was enclosed, in a mixture of tens and fives and singles. There was no message; there was usually no need for the Edinburgh lawyer to have anything special to say. He had simply to disburse in two instalments the two hundred pounds a year that my grand-uncle left me, so that I can live out my life as a gentleman in the great Hall of Torsay.

Thora Garth returned this morning from the senior school in Hamnavoe, at the end of her first session there. I happened to be down at the pier when the weekly mail steamer drew alongside. Several islanders were there, as always on that important occasion. The rope came snaking ashore. A seaman shouted banter to the fishermen and Robbie Tenston the farmer of Dale (who had just come out of the hotel bar). The minister turned away, pretending not to have heard the swear-words. I found Maurice Garth standing beside me. 'What's wrong with the creels today?' I said to him. . . . 'I'm expecting Thora,' Maurice said in that mild shy murmur that many of the islanders have. 'She should be on the boat. It's the summer holidays – she'll be home for seven weeks.'

Sure enough, there was the tilted serious freckled face above the rail. She acknowledged her father with a slight sideways movement of her hand. At that moment I was distracted by an argument that had broken out on the pier. Robbie Tenston of Dale was claiming possession of a large square plywood box that had just been swung ashore from the *Pomona*.

'Nonsense,' cried William Copinsay the general merchant. 'Don't be foolish. It's loaves. It's the bread I always get from the baker in the town on a Friday.'

And indeed – though I hated to agree with Copinsay – there was no doubt that the box contained bread; the incense of new baking drifted across the pier.

'Don't you call me a fool,' said Robbie Tenston in his dark dangerous drinking voice. 'This is a box of plants, if you want to know. It's for my wife's greenhouse. The market gardener wrote to say that it was coming on the boat today. That's why I'm here, man. Let go of it now.'

Copinsay and Robbie Tenston had each laid hands on the rope that was round the box. A circle of onlookers gathered raggedly about them.

The trouble was, the label had somehow got scraped off in transit. (But Robbie must have been stupid to have missed that delicious smell of new rolls and loaves. Besides, roots and greenery would never have weighed so much.)

They wrestled for the box, both of them red in the face. It had all the makings of a disgraceful scene. Four of the crew had stopped working. They watched from the derrick, delighted. The skipper leaned out of his cabin, grinning eagerly. They could have told who owned the box by rights, but they wanted the entertainment to go on for some time yet.

Mr Evelyn the minister attempted to settle the affair. 'Now now,' he said, 'now now – it is simply a matter of undoing the rope – please, Mr Copinsay – Robert, I beg you – and looking inside.'

They paid no attention to him. The farmer dragged the box from the weaker hands of the merchant. Copinsay's face was twisted with rage and spite. 'You old miserly bastard!' shouted Robbie.

The skipper leaned further out of his cabin. He put his pipe carefully on the ledge and clapped his hands. Maggie Swintoun and a few other women came down the pier from their houses, attracted by the hullabaloo.

At that point Copinsay flung himself on Robbie Tenston and began to scratch at his face like a woman. He screamed a few falsetto incoherences.

The dispute had reached a dangerous stage. (I felt that, as the chief man in the island, I should be doing something about it, but I am morbidly afraid of making a fool of myself in front of these people.) Robbie could have taken the merchant in his great earth-red hands and broken him. He could have picked him up and flung him into the sea. He tried first of all to shake himself free from the hysterical clutchings of William Copinsay. He struck Copinsay an awkward blow on the shoulder. They whirled each other round like mad dancers between the horse-box and the gangway. Then – still grappling – they achieved some kind of a stillness; through it they glared at each other.

God knows what might have happened then.

It was Thora Garth who restored peace to the island. It was extraordinary, the way the focus shifted from the two buffoons to the girl. But suddenly everyone on the pier, including the skipper and the fighters and myself, was looking at her alone. She had left the steamer and was standing on the pier beside the disputed box. She had one hand on it, laid flat. With the other she pointed to William Copinsay.

'The box belongs to him,' she said quietly. 'Robbie, the box belongs to Mr Copinsay.'

That was the end of the fracas. Robbie Tenston seemed to accept her verdict at once. He pushed Mr Copinsay away. He muttered a grudging 'Well, don't let him or anybody ever call me a fool again.' He walked up the pier, his face encrimsoned, past Maggie Swintoun and the other women who were flocking to the scene, too late, with their false chorus of commiseration and accusation. 'That Robbie Tenston should be reported to the police,' said Maggie Swintoun flatly. 'It's that pub to blame. It should be closed down. Drink is the cause of all the trouble in Torsay. Them in authority should be doing something about it.'. . . She kept looking at me out of the corner of her eye.

Mr Copinsay sat on his box of bread and began to weep silently.

I could not bear any more of it.

The seamen had returned to their work, swinging ashore mail-bags, crates of beer, saddlery, a bicycle, newspapers. Steve Mack the skipper was lighting his pipe and looking inland to the island hills as if nothing untoward had happened.

I left the women cluck-clucking with sympathy around Copinsay Agonistes. I took my box of books that was sent each month from the library in the town – there was never likely to be any fighting about that piece of cargo – and walked up the pier.

From the gate of The Hall I looked back at the village. Thora Garth was greeting her mother in the open door of their cottage. Maurice carried his daughter's case. The woman and the girl – the one was as tall as the other now – leaned towards each other and kissed briefly. The dog barked and danced around them.

On the top of the island, where the road cuts into the shoulder of the hill, a small dark figure throbbed for a minute against the sky. It was Robbie Tenston bearing his resentment and shame home to Dale.

This evening I called in at the hotel bar for a glass of beer – a thing I rarely do; but it has been, for Orkney, a warm day, and also I must confess I am missing James MacIntosh already – he went home to Perth for the summer vacation two days ago. Seven weeks without chess and argument is a long time.

Maurice Garth was sitting in the window seat drinking stout. I took my glass of beer across to his table.

'Well,' I said, 'and how is Thora liking the big school in Hamnavoe?'

'She isn't clever,' he said, smiling. 'I doubt she won't go very far as a scholar. But what is there for a lass to do in Torsay nowadays? Everybody's leaving the island. I suppose in the end she might get some kind of a job in the town.'

'It was remarkable,' I said, 'the way Thora put a stop to that fight on the pier this morning.'

'Oh, I don't know,' said Maurice. 'The pair of idiots! Any fool could have seen that it was a bread box. I hope we'll hear no more about it. I hope there isn't going to be any trouble about it with the police.'

'They might have done each other an injury,' I said. 'It was your Thora who brought them to their senses. I never saw anything quite so astonishing.'

'No, no,' said Maurice, raising his hand. 'Don't say that. Thora's just an ordinary lass. There's nothing so very strange about it. Thora just pointed out what was what to that pair of fools. Say no more about it.'

Maurice Garth is a placid man. Such vehemence is strange, coming from him. But perhaps it was that he had drunk too many glasses of stout.

There has been a fine morsel of scandal in the village this morning. The Swintoun woman has been going about the doors at all hours, her cheeks aflame with excitement. It seems that the younger son of Wear, the main farm in the island, has been jilted. Everything has been set fair for a wedding for three months past. Consignments of new furniture, carpets, curtains, crockery have been arriving in the steamer from Hamnavoe; to be fetched later the same afternoon by a farm servant in a cart. They do things in style at Wear. The first friends have gone with their gifts, even. I myself wandered about the empty caverns of this house all one morning last week, considering whether this oil painting or that antique vase might be acceptable. The truth is, I can hardly afford any more to give them a present of money. In the end I thought they might be happy with an old silk sampler framed in mahogany that one of my grand-aunts made in the middle of Queen Victoria's reign. It is a beautiful piece of work. At Wear they would expect something new and glittery from the laird. I hoped, however, that the bride might be pleased with my present.

The Rev. Mr Evelyn was going to have made the first proclamation from the pulpit next Sunday morning. (I never attend the church services here myself, being nominally an Episcopalian, like most of the other Orkney lairds.)

Well, the island won't have to worry any more about this particular ceremony, for – so Traill the postman told me over the garden wall this morning – the prospective bride has gone to live in a wooden shack at the other end of the island – a hut left over from the Kaiser's war – with Shaun Midhouse, a deck hand on the *Pomona*, a man of no particular comeliness or gifts – in fact, a rather unprepossessing character – certainly not what the women of Torsay would call 'a good catch', by any means.

I am sorry for Jack Grossiter of Wear. He seems a decent enough young chap, not at all like some others in the household. His father of all men I dislike in Torsay. He is arrogant and overbearing towards those whom he considers his inferiors; but you never saw such cap-raisings and foot-scrapings as when he chances to meet the minister or the schoolmaster or myself on the road. He is also the wealthiest man in the island,

yet the good tilth that he works belongs to me, and I am
forbidden by law to charge more than a derisory rent for it.
I try not to let this curious situation influence me, but of
course it does nothing to sweeten my regard for the man. In
addition to everything else he is an upstart and an ignoramus.
How delighted he was when his only daughter Sophie married
that custom house officer two years ago – that was a feather
in his cap, for according to the curious snobbery of folk like
Grossiter a man who has a pen-and-paper job is a superior
animal altogether to a crofter who labours all his life among
earth and blood and dung. The elder son Andrew will follow
him in Wear, no doubt, for since that piece of socialism was
enacted in parliament in 1882 even death does not break the
secure chain of a family's tenure. . . . For Andrew, in his turn,
a good match was likewise negotiated, no less than Mr Copinsay
the merchant's daughter. Wear will be none the poorer for
that alliance. Only Jack Grossiter remained unmarried. Whom
he took to wife was of comparatively small importance – a
hill croft would be found for him when the time came. I could
imagine well enough the brutish reasonings of the man of
Wear, once his second son began to be shaken with the rud-
diness and restlessness of virility. There was now, for instance,
that bonny respectable well-handed lass in the village – Thora
Garth – what objection could there be to her? She would
make a good wife to any man, though of course her father
was only a fisherman and not over-burdened with wealth.
One afternoon – I can picture it all – the man of Wear would
have said a few words to Maurice Garth in the pub, and bought
him a dram. One evening soon after that Jack Grossiter and
Thora would have been left alone together in the sea-bright
room above the shore; a first few cold words passed between
them. It gradually became known in the village that they
were engaged. I have seen them, once or twice this summer,
walking along the shore together into the sunset.

  Now, suddenly, this has shaken the island.

The first unusual thing to happen was that Thora went missing, one morning last week. She simply walked out of the house with never a word to her parents. There had been no quarrel, so Armingert assured the neighbours. For the first hour or two she didn't worry about Thora; she might have walked up to Wear, or called on Minnie Farquharson who was working on the bridal dress. But she did not come home for her dinner, and that was unusual, that was a bit worrying. Armingert called at this door and that in the afternoon. No-one had seen Thora since morning. Eventually it was Benny Smith the ferryman who let out the truth, casually, to Maurice Garth, at the end of the pier, when he got back from Hamnavoe in the early evening. He had taken Thora across in his boat the *Lintie* about ten o'clock that morning. She hadn't said a word to him all the way across. It wasn't any concern of his, and anyway she wasn't the kind of young woman who likes her affairs to be known.

Well, that was a bit of a relief to Maurice and Armingert. They reasoned that Thora must suddenly have thought of some necessary wedding purchase; she would be staying overnight with one of her Hamnavoe friends (one of the girls she had been to school with); she would be back on the *Pomona* the next morning.

And in fact she did come back on Friday on board the *Pomona*. She walked at once from the boat to her parents' door. Who was trailing two paces behind her but Shaun Midhouse, one of the crew of the *Pomona*? Thora opened the cottage door and went inside (Shaun lingered at the gate). She told her mother – Maurice was at the lobsters – that she could not marry Jack Grossiter of Wear after all, because she had discovered that she liked somebody else much better. There was a long silence in the kitchen. Then her mother asked who this other man was. Thora pointed through the window. The deck-hand was shuffling about on the road outside with that hangdog look that he has when he isn't working or drinking.

'That's my man,' Thora said – 'I'm going to live with him.'
Armingert said that she would give much pain and grief to
those near to her if she did what she said she was going to do.
Thora said she realized that. 'I'm sorry,' she said. Then she
left the cottage and walked up the brae to the farm of Wear.
Shaun went a few paces with her through the village, but left
her outside the hotel and went back on board the *Pomona*;
the boat was due to sail again in ten minutes.

Thora wouldn't go into the farmhouse. She said what she
had to say standing in the door, and it only lasted a minute.
Then she turned and walked slowly across the yard to the
road. The old man went a few steps after her, shouting and
shaking his fists. His elder son Andrew called him back,
coldly – his father musn't make a fool of himself before the
whole district. Let the slut go. His father must remember that
he was the most important farmer in Torsay.

Jack had already taken his white face from the door – it
hasn't been seen anywhere in the island since. I am deeply
sorry for him.

I ought to go along and see these people. God knows what
I can say to them. I am hopeless in such situations. I was not
created to be a bringer of salves and oils.

I saw the minister coming out of the farmhouse two day
ago. . . .

The eastern part of the island is very desolate, scarred with
peat-bogs and Pictish burial places. During the war the army
built an artillery battery on the links there. (They com-
mandeered the site – my subsequent granting of permission
was an empty token.) All that is left of the camp now, among
concrete foundations, is a single wooden hut that had been
the officers' mess. No-one has lived there since 1919 – inside
it must be all dampness and mildew. Tom Christianson the
shepherd saw, two days after the breaking of the engagement,
smoke coming from the chimney of the hut. He kept an eye
on the place; later that afternoon a van drove up; Shaun

Midhouse carried from van to hut a mattress, a sack of coal, a box of groceries. He reported the facts to me. That night, late, I walked between the hills and saw a single lamp burning in the window.

Thora Garth and Shaun Midhouse have been living there for a full week now – as Mr Copinsay the merchant says, 'in sin'; managing to look, as he says it, both pained and pleased.

Two nights ago Armingert and Maurice came to see me.

'Shaun Midhouse is such a poor weed of a creature,' said Armingert in my cold library. 'What ever could any girl see in the likes of *that*?'

Maurice shook his head. They are, both these dear folk, very troubled.

'Jack Grossiter is ill,' said Armingert. 'I never saw a boy so upset. I am very very sorry for him.'

'I will go and see him tomorrow,' I said.

'What trouble she has caused,' said Armingert. 'I did not think such a thing was possible. If she had suddenly attacked us with a knife it would have been easier to bear. She is a bad cruel deceptive girl.'

'She is our daughter,' said Maurice gently.

'We have no business to inflict our troubles on you,' said Armingert. 'What we have come about is this, all the same. We understand that you own that war-time site. They are sitting unbidden in your property, Thora and that creature. That is what it amounts to. You could evict them.'

I shook my head.

'You could have the law on them,' she insisted. 'You could force them out. She would have to come home then, if you did that. That would bring her to her senses.'

'I'm sorry,' I said. 'There is something at work here that none of us understands, some kind of an elemental force. It is terrible and it is delicate at the same time. It must work itself out in Thora and Shaun Midhouse. I am not wise enough to interfere.'

There was silence in the library for a long time after that. Armingert looked hurt and lost. No doubt but she is offended with me.

'He is right,' said Maurice at last. 'She is our daughter. We must just try to be patient.'

Then they both got to their feet. They looked tired and sad. They who had been childless for so long in their youth are now childless again; and they are growing old; and an area of their life where there was nothingness twenty years ago is now all vivid pain.

I knew it would happen some day: that old school-house dog has savaged one of the islanders, and a child at that. I was in the garden, filling a bowl with gooseberries, when I heard the terrible outcry from the village, a mingling of snarls and screams. 'Joe, you brute!' came James MacIntosh's voice (it was a still summer evening; every sound carried for miles) – 'Bad dog! Get into the house this minute!'...And then in a soothing voice, 'Let's see your leg then. It's only a graze, Mansie. You got a fright, that's all....That bad Joe....Shush now, no need to kick up such a row. You'll deafen the whole village.'...This Mansie, whoever he was, refused to be comforted. The lamentation came nearer. I heard the school-house door being banged shut (my garden wall is too high to see the village): James MacIntosh had gone indoors, possibly to chastise his cur. Presently a boy, sobbing and snivelling in spasms, appeared on the road. He leaned against a pillar to get his breath. 'Hello,' I said, 'would you like some gooseberries?'

Greed and self-pity contended in Mansie's face. He unlatched the gate and came in, limping. There was a livid crescent mark below his knee. He picked a fat gooseberry from my bowl. He looked at it wonderingly. His lips were still shivering with shock.

'That damn fool of a dog,' I said. 'Did he seize you then? You'd better come into the kitchen. I'll put some disinfectant on it. I have bandages.'

The cupped palm of his hand brimmed with gooseberries. He bit into several, one after the other, with a half-reluctant lingering relish. Then he crammed six or seven into his mouth till his cheek bulged. His brown eyes dissolved in rapture; he closed them; there was a runnel of juice from one corner of his mouth to his chin.

The day was ending in a riot of colour westward. Crimson and saffron and jet the sea blazed, like stained glass.

'The disinfectant,' I said. 'It's in the kitchen.'

He balanced the last of the gooseberries on the tip of his tongue, rolled it round inside his mouth, and bit on it. 'It's nothing,' he said. 'I was in the village visiting my grand-da. It was me to blame really. I kicked Joe's bone at the school gate. I must be getting home now. Thora'll be wondering about me.'. . .

So, he was one of the Midhouse boys. He looked like neither of his parents. He had the shy swift gentle eyes of Maurice his grandfather. He relished gooseberries the way that old Maurice sipped his stout in the hotel bar.

'And anyway,' he said, 'I wouldn't come into your house to save my life.'

'What's wrong with my house?' I said.

'It's the laird's house,' he said. 'It's The Hall. I'm against all that kind of thing. I'm a communist.' (He was maybe ten years old.)

'There isn't anything very grand about this great ruckle of stones,' I said. 'It's falling to pieces. You should see the inside of it. Just look at this wilderness of a garden. I'll tell you the truth, Mansie – I'm nearly as poor as Ezra the tinker. So come in till I fix your leg.'

He shook his head. 'It's the principle of it,' said Mansie. 'You oppressed my ancestors. You taxed them to death. You drove them to Canada and New Zealand. You made them work in your fields for nothing. They built this house for you, yes, and their hands were red carrying up stones from the shore. I wouldn't go through your door for a pension. What does one man want with a big house like this anyway? Thora and me and my brothers live in two small rooms up at Solsetter.'

'I'm sorry, Mansie,' I said. 'I promise I won't ever be wicked like that again. But I am worried about that bite on your leg.'

'It's the same with the kirk,' said Mansie. 'Do you think I could have just one more gooseberry? I would never enter that kirk door. All that talk about sin and hell and angels. Do you know what I think about the bible? It's one long fairy-tale from beginning to end. I'm an atheist, too. You can tell the minister what I said if you like. I don't care. I don't care for any of you.'

The rich evening light smote the west gable of The Hall. The great house took, briefly, a splendour. The wall flushed and darkened. Then with all its withered stonework and ramshackle rooms it began to enter the night.

The gooseberry bush twanged. The young anarchist was plucking another fruit.

'I don't believe in anything,' he said. 'Nothing at all. You are born. You live for a while. Then you die. My grandma died last year. Do you know what she is now? Dust in the kirkyard. They could have put her in a ditch, it would have been all the same. When you're dead you're dead.'

'You'd better be getting home then, comrade, before it's dark,' I said.

'Do you know this,' he said, 'I have no father. At least, I do have a father but he doesn't live with us any more. He went away one day, suddenly. Oh, a while ago now, last winter. Jock Ritch saw him once in Falmouth. He was on a trawler. We don't know where he is. I'm glad he's gone. I didn't like him. And I'll tell you another thing.'

'Tomorrow,' I said. 'You must go home now. You must get that bite seen to. If you don't, some day there'll be an old man hobbling round this village with a wooden leg. And it'll be you, if you don't show that wound to your mother right away.'

'Rob and Willie and me,' he said, 'we're bastards. I bet I've shocked you. I bet you think I said a bad word. You see, Thora was never married. Thora, she's my mother. I suppose you would say "illegitimate" but it's just the same thing. The gooseberries were good. They're not your gooseberries though. They belong to the whole island by rights. I was only taking my share.'

The darkness had come down so suddenly that I could not say when the boy left my door. I was aware only that one smell had been subtracted from the enchanting cluster of smells that gather about an island on a late summer evening. A shadow was gone from the garden. I turned and went inside, carrying the bowl of gooseberries. (There would be one pot of jam less next winter.) I traversed, going to the kitchen, a corridor with an ancient ineradicable sweetness of rot in it.

I have been ill, it seems. I still feel like a ghost in a prison of bone. I have been very ill, James MacIntosh says. 'I thought you were for the kirkyard,' he told me last night. 'That's the truth. I thought an ancient proud island family was guttering out at last.'...He said after a time, 'There's something tough about you, man. I think you'll see the boots off us all.' He put the kettle on my fire to make a pot of tea. 'I don't suppose now,' he said, 'that you'll be up to a game of chess just yet. Quite so.' He is a sweet considerate man. 'I'll fill your hot-water bottle before I go,' he said, 'it's very cold up in that bedroom.'

The whole house is like a winter labyrinth in the heart of this summer-time island. It is all this dampness and rot, I'm sure, that made me so ill last month. The Hall is withering slowly about me. I cannot afford now to re-slate the roof. There is warping and woodworm and patches of damp every-where. The three long corridors empty their overplus of draught into every mildewed bedroom. Even last October, when the men from the fishing boat broke the billiard-room window, going between the hotel and the barn dance at Dale, I had to go without tobacco for a fortnight or so until the joiner was paid. Not much can be done these days on two hundred pounds a year.

'James,' I said, 'I'm going to shift out of that bedroom. Another winter there and I'd be a gonner. I wonder if I could get a small bed fitted into some corner of the kitchen – over there, for example, out of the draught. I don't mind eating and sleeping in the same room.'

This morning (Saturday) MacIntosh came up from the school-house with a small iron folding bed. 'It's been in the outhouse since I came to Torsay,' he said. 'The last teacher must have had it for one of his kids. It's a bit rusty, man, but it's sound, perfectly sound. Look for yourself. If you'll just shift that heap of books out of the corner I'll get it fixed up in no time.'. . . .

We drank some tea while blankets and pillows were airing at the kitchen fire. I tried to smoke my pipe but the thing tasted foul – the room plunged; there was a blackness before my eyes; I began to sweat. 'You're not entirely well yet by any means,' said the schoolmaster. 'Put that pipe away. It'll be a week or two before you can get over the door, far less down to the hotel for a pint. I'm telling you, you've been very ill. You don't seem to realize how desperate it was with you. But for one thing only you'd be in the family vault.'

People who have been in the darkness for a while long to know how it was with them when they were no longer there to observe and evaluate. They resent their absence from the dear ecstatic flesh; they suspect too that they may have been caught out by their attendants in some weakness or shame that they themselves make light of, or even indulge, in the ordinary round. At the same time there is a kind of vanity in sickness. It sets a person apart from the folk who only eat and sleep and sorrow and work. Those dullards become the servants of the hero who has ventured into the shadowy border-land next to the kingdom of death – the sickness bestows a special quality on him, a seal of gentility almost. There are people who wear their scars and pock-marks like decorations. The biography of such a one is a pattern of small sicknesses, until at last the kingdom he has fought against and been fascinated with for so long besets him with irresistible steel and fire. There is one last trumpet call under a dark tower. . . .

This afternoon, by means of subtle insistent questions, I got from James MacIntosh the story of my trouble. He would much rather have been sitting with me in amiable silence over a chessboard. I knew of course the beginning of the story; how I had had to drag myself about the house for some days at the end of May with a gray quake on me. To get potatoes from the garden – a simple job like that – was a burdensome penance. The road to the village and the tobacco jar on Mr Copinsay's shelf was a wearisome 'via crucis', but at last I could not even get that far. My pipe lay cold on the window-sill for two days. Sometime during the third day the sun became a blackness.

'Pneumonia,' said James MacIntosh. 'That's what it was. Dr Wayne stood in the school-house door and barked at me. *The laird up yonder, your friend, he has double pneumonia. By rights he should be in the hospital in Kirkwall. That's out of the question, he's too ill. He'll have to bide where he is. . . Now then* (says he) *there's not a hell of a lot I can do for him. That's the truth. It's a dicey thing, pneumonia. It comes to a crisis. The sick man reaches a crossroads, if you understand what I mean. He lingers there for an hour or two. Then he simply goes one way or the other. There's no telling. What is essential though* (says the old quack) *is good nursing. There must be somebody with him night and day – two, if possible, one to relieve the other. Now then, you must know some woman or other in the island who has experience of this kind of thing. Get her. . . .* And out of the house he stumps with his black bag, down the road, back to the ferry-boat at the pier.

'So there you lay, in that great carved mahogany bed upstairs, sweating and raving. Old Wayne had laid the responsibility fairly and squarely on me. I had to get a nurse. But what nurse? And where? The only person who does any kind of nursing in the island is that Maggie Swintoun – at least, she brings most of the island bairns into the world, and it's her they generally send for when anybody dies. But nursing – I never actually heard of her attending sick folk. And besides, I knew you disliked the woman. If you were to open your eyes and see that face at the foot of the bed it would most likely, I thought, be the end of you. But that didn't prevent Mistress Swintoun from offering her services that same day. There she stood, keening and whispering at the foot of the stair – she had had the impudence to come in without knocking. *I hear the laird isn't well, the poor man* (says she). *Well now, if there's anything I can do. I don't mind sitting up all night.* . . . And the eyes of her going here and there over the portraits in the staircase and over all the silver plate in the hall-stand. *Thank you all the same,* said I, *but other arrangements have been made* . . . . Off she went then, like a cat leaving a fish on a doorstep. I was worried all the same, I can tell you. I went down to the village to have a consultation with Minnie Farquharson the seamstress. She knows everybody in Torsay, what they can do and what they can't do. She demurred. In the old days there would have been no difficulty: the island was teeming with kindly capable women who would have been ideal for the job. But things are different now, Minnie pointed out. Torsay is half empty. Most of the houses are in ruin. The young women are away in the towns, working in shops and offices. All that's left in the way of women-folk are school bairns and "puir auld bodies". She honestly couldn't think of a single suitable person. *"Now* (says she) *I doubt you'll have to put an advertisement in "The Orcadian".'*

'I knew, as I walked back up the brae, that by the time the advertisement – "Wanted, experienced private nurse to attend gentleman" – had appeared, and been answered, and the nurse interviewed and approved and brought over to Torsay, there would have been no patient for her to attend to. The marble jaws would have swallowed you up. . . .

'When I turned in at the gate of The Hall, I saw washed sheets and pillow-cases hanging in the garden, between the potato patch and the gooseberry bushes, where no washing has ever flapped in the wind for ten years and more. (You hang your shirts and socks, I know, in front of the stove.) I went into the house. The fire was lit in the kitchen. The windows along the corridor were open, and there was a clean sweet air everywhere instead of those gray draughts. I'm not a superstitious man, but I swear my hand was shaking when I opened the door of your bedroom. And there she was, bent over you and putting cold linen to the beaded agony on your face.'

'Who?' I said.

'And there she stayed for ten days, feeding you, washing you, comforting you, keeping the glim of life in you night and day. Nobody ever relieved her. God knows when she slept. She was never, as far as I could make out, a minute away from your room. But of course she must have been, to cook, wash, prepare the medicines, things like that. She had even set jars of flowers in odd niches and corners. The house began to smell fragrant.'

I said, 'Yes, but who?'

'She told me, standing there in your bedroom that first day, that I didn't need to worry any longer. She thought she could manage. What could I do anyway, she said, with the school bairns to teach from ten in the morning till four in the afternoon? And she smiled at me, as though there was some kind of conspiracy between us. And she nodded, half in dismissal and half in affirmation. I went down that road to the school-house with a burden lifted from me, I can tell you. *Well, if he doesn't get better*, I thought, *it won't be for want of a good nurse*.'

'You haven't told me her name,' I said.

'On the Thursday old Wayne came out of The Hall shaking

his head. I saw him from the school window. He was still shaking his head when he stepped on board the *Lintie* at the pier. That was the day of the crisis. I ran up to your house as soon as the school was let out at half past three (for I couldn't bear to wait till four o'clock). The flame was gulping in the lamp all right. Your pulse had no cohesion or rhythm. There were great gaps in your breathing. I stood there, expecting darkness and silence pretty soon. What is it above all that a woman gives to a man? God knows. Some strong pure dark essence of the earth that seems not to be a part of the sun-loving clay of men at all. The woman was never away from your bedside that night. I slept, on and off, between two chairs in the kitchen. At sunrise next morning you spoke for the first time for, I think, twelve days. You asked for – of all things – a cup of tea. But the nurse, she was no longer there.'

'For God's sake,' I said, 'tell me who she is.'

'You'll have to be doing with my crude services,' said James MacIntosh, 'till you're able to do for yourself. You should be out and about in a week, if this good weather holds. I thought I told you who she was.'

'You didn't,' I said.

'Well now,' he said, 'I thought I did. It was Thora Garth, of course.'

This morning I had a visit from a young man I have never seen before. It turns out that he is a missionary, a kind of lay Presbyterian preacher. There has been no minister in Torsay since the Rev. Mr Evelyn retired three years ago; the spiritual needs of the few people remaining have been attended to, now and then, by ministers from other islands.

This missionary is an earnest young bachelor. He has a sense of vocation but no humour. Someone in the village must have told him about me. 'Mister, you'd better call on the old man up at The Hall. You'll likely be able to understand the posh way he speaks. He only manages down to the village once a week nowadays for his tobacco and his margarine and his loaf. He has nothing to live on but an annuity – nowadays, with the price of things, it would hardly keep a cat. The likes of him is too grand of course to apply for Social Security. God knows what way he manages to live at all. He's never been a church man, but I'm sure he'd be pleased to see an educated person like you.'...I can just imagine Andrew Grossiter, or one of the other elders, saying that to the newcomer some Sunday morning after the service, pointing up the brae to the big house with the fallen slates and the broken sundial.

So, here he was, this young preacher, come to visit me out of Christian duty. He put on me a bright kind smile from time to time.

'I like it here, in Torsay,' he said. 'Indeed I do. It's a great change from the city. I expect it'll take me a wee while to get used to country ways. I come from Glasgow myself. For example, I'm as certain as can be that someone has died in the village this morning. I saw a man carrying trestles into one of the houses. There was a coffin in the back of his van. By rights I should have been told about it at once. It's my duty to visit the bereaved relatives. I'll be wanted of course for the funeral. Ah well, I'll make enquiries this afternoon sometime.'

He eyed with a kind of innocent distaste the sole habitable room left in my house, the kitchen. If I had known he was coming I might have tidied the place up a bit. But for the sake of truth it's best when visitors come unexpectedly on the loaf and cracked mug on the table, the unmade bed, the webbed windows, and all the mingled smells of aged bachelordom.

'Death is a common thing in Torsay nowadays,' I said. 'Nearly everybody left in the village is old. There's hardly a young person in the whole island except yourself.'

'I hope you don't mind my visiting you,' said the missionary. 'I understand you're an episcopalian. These days we must try to be as ecumenical as we can. Now sir, please don't be offended at what I'm going to say. It could be that, what with old age and the fact that you're not so able as you used to be, you find yourself with less money than you could be doing with – for example, to buy a bag of coal or a bit of butcher-meat.'

'I manage quite well,' I said. 'I have an annuity from my grand-uncle. I own this house. I don't eat a great deal.'

'Quite so,' he said. 'But the cost of everything keeps going up. Your income hardly covers the little luxuries that make life a bit more bearable. Now, I've been looking through the local church accounts and I've discovered that there are one or two small bequests that I have the disposal of. I don't see why you shouldn't be a beneficiary. They're for every poor person in the island, whatever church he belongs to, or indeed if he belongs to no church at all.'

'I don't need a thing,' I said.

'Well,' he said, 'if ever you feel like speaking to me about it. The money is there. It's for everybody in Torsay who needs it.'

'Torsay will soon require nothing,' I said.

'I must go down to the village now and see about this death,' he said. 'I noticed three young men in dark suits coming off the *Pomona* this morning. They must be relatives of some kind. . . . I'll find my own way out. Don't bother. This is a fascinating old house right enough. These stones, if only they could speak. God bless you, now.'

He left me then, that earnest innocent young man. I was glad in a way to see the back of him – though I liked him well enough – for I was longing for a pipeful of tobacco, and I'm as certain as can be that he is one of those evangelicals who disapprove of smoking and drinking.

So, there is another death in the island. Month by month Torsay is re-entering the eternal loneliness and silence. The old ones die. The young ones go away to farm in other places, or to car factories in Coventry or Bathgate. The fertile end of the island is littered with roofless windowless crofts. Sometimes, on a fine afternoon, I take my stick and walk for an hour about my domain. Last week I passed Dale, which Robbie Tenston used to farm. (He has been in Australia for fifteen years.) I pushed open the warped door of the dwelling-house. A great gray ewe lurched past me out of the darkness and nearly knocked me over. Birds whirred up through the bare rafters. There were bits of furniture here and there – a table, a couple of chairs, a wooden shut-bed. A framed photograph of the Channel Fleet still hung at the damp wall. There were empty bottles and jam jars all over the floor among sheep-turds and bird-splashes. . . . Most of the farm houses in Torsay are like that now.

It is an island dedicated to extinction. I can never imagine young people coming back to these uncultivated fields and eyeless ruins. Soon now, I know, the place will be finally abandoned to gulls and crows and rabbits. When first I came to Torsay fifty years ago, summoned from London by my grand-uncle's executor, I could still read the heraldry and the Latin motto over the great Hall door. There is a vague shape on the sandstone lintel now; otherwise it is indecipherable. All that style and history and romance have melted back into the stone.

Life in a flourishing island is a kind of fruitful interweaving music of birth and marriage and death: a trio. The old pass mildly into the darkness to make way for their bright grand-children. There is only one dancer in the island now and he carries the hour-glass and the spade and the scythe.

How many have died in the past few years? I cannot re-member all the names. The severest loss, as far as I am con-cerned, is James MacIntosh. The school above the village closed ten years ago, when the dominie retired. There were not enough pupils to justify a new teacher. He did not want to leave Torsay – his whole life was entirely rooted here. He loved the trout fishing, and our chess and few drams twice a week; he liked to follow the careers of his former pupils in every part of the world – he had given so much of his life to them. What did he know of his few remaining relatives in

Perthshire? 'Here I am and here I'll bide,' he said to me the day the school closed. I offered him a croft a mile away – Unibreck – that had just been vacated: the young crofter had got a job in an Edinburgh brewery. James MacIntosh lived there for two winters, reading his 'Forward' and working out chess moves from the manual he kept beside his bed....One morning Maggie Swintoun put her head in at my kitchen door when I was setting the fire. 'O sir,' she wailed, 'a terrible thing has happened!' Every broken window, every winter cough, every sparrow-fall was stuff of tragedy to Maggie Swintoun. I didn't bother even to look round at the woman – I went on laying a careful stratum of sticks on the crumpled paper. 'Up at Unibreck,' she cried, 'your friend, poor Mr MacIntosh the teacher. I expected it. He hasn't been looking well this past month and more.'...She must have been put out by the coal-blackened face I turned on her, for she went away without rounding off her knell. I gathered later that the postman, going with a couple of letters to the cottage, had found James MacIntosh cold and silent in his armchair....I know he would have liked to be buried in Torsay. Those same relatives that he had had no communication with for a quarter of a century ordered his body to be taken down to Dundee. There he was burned in a crematorium and his dust thrown among alien winds.

Maggie Swintoun herself is a silence about the doors of the village. Her ghost is there, a shivering silence, between the sea and the hill. In no long time now that frail remembered keen will be lost in the greater silence of Torsay.

The shutters have been up for two years in the general store. William Copinsay was summoned by a stroke one winter evening from his money bags. They left him in the kirkyard, with pennies for eyes, to grope his way towards that unbearable treasure that is laid up (some say) for all who have performed decent acts of charity in their lives; the acts themselves, sub-tleties and shadows and gleams in time being (they say again) but fore-reflections of that hoarded perdurable reality. (I do not believe this myself. I believe in the 'twelve winds' of Housman that assemble the stuff of life for a year or two and then disperse it again.) Anyway, William Copinsay is dead.

Grossiter died at the auction mart in Hamnavoe, among the beasts and the whisky-smelling farmers, one Wednesday afternoon last spring.

Of course I know who has died in Torsay today. I knew hours before that young missionary opened his mouth. I had seen the lamp burning in a window at the end of the village at two o'clock in the morning.

It is not the old man who has died, either. His death could not have given me this unutterable grief that I felt then, and still feel. The heart of the island has stopped beating. I am the laird of a place that has no substance or meaning any more.

I will go down to the cottage sometime today. I will knock at the door. I will ask for permission to look into that still face.

The only child I have had has been taken from me; the only woman I could ever have loved; the only dust that I wished my own dust to be mingled with.

But in the fifty years that Thora Garth and I have lived in this island together we have never exchanged one word.

THE BURNING HARP

A STORY FOR THE EIGHTIETH BIRTHDAY OF NEIL GUNN

Two nights before Yule in the year 1135 a farmer called Olaf and his wife Asleif and all their household were sitting at supper in their house at Duncansby in Caithness, when a kitchen girl looked up and said that there was a fire in the thatch. They all looked up; the roof was burning. Then Anna a dairy girl pointed; the window was all flame and smoke. 'We should leave the house now,' said Olaf. 'We are not going to die of cold, that much is sure,' said his wife Asleif. The door was two red crackling posts and a crazy yellow curtain.

'I think we are having visitors for Yule,' said an old plough-man who was sitting with an ale-horn in the corner. 'I am too old for such boisterous guests. I think I will go to bed.' While the women ran from wall to wall yelling the old ploughman stretched himself out on a bench and seemed to go to sleep. Olaf and Asleif kissed each other in the centre of the room. 'I am glad of one thing,' said Olaf, 'our son Sweyn is out fishing in the Pentland Firth.'

The whole gable end of the house burst into flames.

Outside there was snow on the ground and beyond the burning house it was very dark. A dozen men one by one threw their torches into the rooted blaze. They took out their daggers and axes in case anyone should try to escape from the fire. A thousand sparks flew about like bees and died in the white midden and the long blue ditch.

A man called Ragnar said, 'There are innocent ones inside, servants and children. We have no quarrel with them. They should be let out.'

Oliver threw a bucket of water over the door. He shouted, 'Servants of Olaf, and any children, you are to come out now.'

A few girls ran out into the night with glaring eyes and rushed past the besiegers and were lost in the darkness beyond. A boy came out. He turned and looked back at the fire once, then he ran laughing after the servants, rising and falling in the snow, wild with excitement.

'I don't think we should have done that,' said Nord. 'These servants will tell the story of the burning all over Caithness. You know how women exaggerate. People here and there will think poorly of us for this night's work. That boy will grow up and remember the burning.'

Now that the girls were out of the house all was much quieter inside. Even the tumult of the flames was stilled a little. In the silence they heard the sound of a voice praying.

'Valt the priest is inside,' said Oliver. 'I had forgotten that he might be here at this time of year. We would not be very popular with the bishop or the monks if Valt were to die. Throw another bucket of water at the door.'

Father Valt came out with a scorched cross between his fingers. There was soot in his beard. He said to Oliver and the other besiegers, 'God pity you, my poor children.' Then he turned and absolved the dead and the dying inside, and walked away slowly towards the church at the shore.

'We didn't get much gratitude out of that priest,' said Nord. 'In my opinion it was a mistake to let a man like that go. With Father Valt it will be hell-fire for all us burners from now until the day he is able to preach no more. We will have no comfort at all, standing in his kirk.'

They heard a few faint harp-strokes through the snorings and belchings of flame.

'It is my opinion,' said Ragnar, 'that there is a poet inside.'

'Well,' said Nord, 'what is a poet more than a miller or a fisherman or a blacksmith?'

'From the sound of the harp,' said Oliver, 'from the way it is being played, it seems to me that the poet in there is none other than Niall from Dunbeath.'

'Well,' said Nord, 'and what about it? What is Niall more than other string-pluckers, Angus say, or Keld, or Harald?'

'Nord,' said Oliver, 'you are very thick in the head. I would keep my mouth shut. Niall is the poet who made the ballad of the silver shoals in the west. He also sang about the boy and the fishing boat – if I am not mistaken that was the first story he told. He was the one too who made us aware of the mysterious well of wisdom. He made that great song about the salmon.'

'It would be a pity indeed, I suppose,' said Nord, 'if the harp of a man like that was to be reduced to a cinder.'

'Nobody in Scotland sings with such purity and sweetness as Niall,' said Oliver. 'We would be shamed for ever if we stopped such a mouth with ashes. The world, we are told, will end in this way, some day soon, in ice and fire and darkness. But how can a harp stroke given to the wind ever perish, even though there are no men left on earth? The gods will hear that music with joy for ever.'

So another bucket of water was thrown over the threshold and the name of the poet Niall was called into the red-and-black dapple inside. Presently an old serene man carrying a harp walked from the burning house into the snow. He seemed not to see the lurid faces all about the door. Honoured, he sought the starlit darkness beyond the lessening circles of flame.

THE TARN AND THE ROSARY

I

HE was cast out of unremembered dark into salt, light, shifting immensities. A woman closed him in with hills, sweet waters, biddings, bodings, thunders and dewfalls of love. He sat among three sisters and one brother at a scrubbed table. Colm: that was his name. There were small noises from a new cradle in the corner. His mother was a little removed from him then. His father was in the west since morning. The cow Flos that belonged to the croft next door bent and nuzzled buttercups. Hens screeched round a shower of oats from old Merran's fist. A gentleness of beard and eyes came in at the door at thickening light with fish and an oar: his father. Then his mother and brother and three sisters and the old one went silently to their different places. The infant, Ellen, was lifted from cradle to breast. The lamp was lit. His father wiped plate with crust. His father filled his pipe. His father spoke from the chair beside the smoke and flame. His father opened a book. There was a silence. The boy closed his eyes. Then very ancient wisdom was uttered upon the house, a gentle deliberate voice prayed from the armchair: his grandfather.

2

In the wide grassy playground the children whirled and chirruped and slouched. A whistle shrieked: the children were enchanted to silence. They stepped quietly past the teacher into a huge gloom, desks and globe and blackboard. Miss Silver said, more grave than any elder, 'A terrible thing has happened, a sum of money has been removed from my purse this morning. This is what must happen now. You will all empty your pockets on to your desks, every single thing, and then we will see who took the half-crown and the two sixpences. . . .' Guilt whitened Colm's face like chalk (though he had done nothing). Soon the desks were strewn with bits of string, shells, fluff, cocoa tin lids, broken blades. Miss Silver strode among all his bruck, jerking her head back and fore like a bird. 'Very well,' she said. 'The thief has hidden his ill-gotten gains. It is now a matter for the police. The policeman will be taking the boat from Hamnavoe tomorrow, with a warrant, and also handcuffs, I have no doubt.' Colm felt like a person diseased, scabbed all over with coins, so that everyone could see he was the culprit (though he had only once seen a half-crown, between his father's fingers, the day his father opened his tin box to pay the rent; a white heavy rich round thing). 'We are doing the exports and imports of Mexico, I think,' said Miss Silver in a hurt voice, turning to the senior class. The school was a place of chastity and awe all that afternoon – the brand of crime was burned on it. . . . 'I wonder if Jackie Hay will be long in jail?' said Andrick Overton on the way home from school. Torquil, Colm's brother, asked why. A surge of joy went through the boy because it was not being said among the pupils that he and only he was the thief. 'Did you see Jackie's mouth when the teacher was searching the desks?' said Andrick. 'He had slack silver teeth.' The older boys all laughed on the road, and Colm laughed too. The Hamnavoe policeman did not come and Jackie Hay was not sent to prison. Instead he bought the big boys who were with him lucky-bags and liquorice sticks next day, Saturday, from the grocery van. He smoked a packet of woodbines himself and was sick in a ditch. Nobody was sorry for Jackie Hay. Torquil's mouth was black and sweet all that afternoon.

3

Colm came through the village carrying a basket of eggs and a pail of buttermilk from the farm of Wardings. 'What a kind body the wife of Wardings is,' his mother always said, her voice going

gentle and wondering. It was true; he liked going to the farm
for the eggs and kirned-milk on a Saturday morning. Mrs
Sanderson always took him in and gave him a thick slice of the
gingerbread she had baked herself. She asked him questions
about the school and his family in a hearty voice. She didn't
seem to mind if some golden crumbs fell from his mouth on to
her stone floor which was always so clean. The door into the
whitewashed kitchen would open for sure, sometime when he
was eating the gingerbread, and the dog come in. He didn't
like dogs. He was nervous of dogs. But Rastus, the black-and-
white collie, seemed to have some share in the kindliness and
benevolence of Wardings. Boy and dog, after the first unsure
moment, eyed each other trustfully. He patted the neck of the
dog (but still with some reserve). Rastus licked the sweet crumbs
from the fingers of his other hand. 'Mrs Sanderson,' he said,
'I'll have to be going now.' . . . Smiling, she stood in the door
and waved goodbye to him.

It was steep, the road down through the village. One terrible
morning, when he was five, he had fallen; every single egg was
smashed and the buttermilk was spilt; red and grey tatters
across the frosty road. He ran home yelling, empty-handed.
He would not even go back to get the pail and the basket.
Mary-Anne had to go and fetch them.

Today he stepped easily down the brae, holding the pail in
one hand and the basket in the other. So delicate his going that
the buttermilk only, at most, shivered into circles. It was
pleasant, the dark rich tang of the gingerbread in his mouth.
Mrs Sanderson was nice. He wouldn't mind biding at a farm
like Wardings.

Huge strength and power broke the skyline. Tom Sanderson
the farmer was ploughing the high field with his team. He
shouted to Colm and waved his arm. Colm waved back.

It was dinner-time, surely. There was not a soul in the village
street. The smell of mince and boiled cabbage came from the
Eunsons' house; that made him feel hungry. The only living

thing on the road was the merchant's dog, Solomon – a lion-coloured mongrel – and it lay asleep in the sun under a window with loaves and cream cookies and one iced cake in it. A bare curved knuckle-ended bone lay at the dog's unconscious head. Whose birthday was it? Colm looked through the shop window at the cake. It must be a boy or girl from one of the better-off families – from the Bu farm, maybe, or the manse, or the doctor's. From the house above the shop came the rattle of plates, a shred of vapour, a most delicious smell of frying onions. His dinner would be ready too, he must hurry. There was no candle – it was more likely to be a christening cake. With his left foot he eased the bone towards the wet black nose. The bone whispered in the dust. A name was written in pink icing on the white-iced cake: *Christopher Albert Marcusson*. That must be the minister's new baby. There would be marzipan inside, spices, sherry, raisins, threepenny bits. The tawny flank heaved once, gently. Sweetness, sweetness. Colm loved all sweet things – languors and dissolvings and raptures in the hot cave of the mouth. The road swirled. His left leg was draped in rage. Teeth and eyes flashed under him, and fell away. Two livid punctured curves converged along his left thigh; they began to leak; his knee was tattered with blood. He set the eggs down carefully on the road; the buttermilk quivered once and was still. The dog skulked across the road to the tailor shop; and it looked back at him once or twice balefully. He looked down at the lacerated leg. It was very strange, his leg wasn't sore at all. On the contrary, it felt warm and pleasant and refreshed (like when you draw it out of a cold pool and let it dry in the sun). Yet he had been bitten. The merchant's dog had bitten him. Nobody had seen it happen. His lip quivered. He picked up the basket and the pail and went slowly, limping, through the dinner-time village to the house at the shore. There was really no need to limp at all, but he limped. It was terrible – he had tried to be good to the dog, to put his bone near his mouth seeing that it was dinner-time, and this was the way the beast had repaid him. His throat worked, and he felt tears in his eyes. There was a numbness now in his thigh. He hurried on. His father was sitting on the wall smoking his after-dinner pipe. Some buttermilk slopped over, the eggs clacked gently. He sobbed. His father looked at him and said, 'You're late for your dinner,' and then saw with astonishment that something was wrong. Colm set down pail and basket on the flat quernstone at the door and with one loud wail flung himself into the fragrant gloom of the kitchen, and the startled faces, and the warm enfolding arms of his mother. He hid the mask of tears in her bosom. He held up his wounded leg. His mother said, 'There there' and 'Poor angel,' and set him down on a chair. His mother issued calm orders: kettle on fire, a bandage, lysol. His three sisters dispersed about these tasks. 'That dog of Wardings,' said his mother. 'What do they call him, Rastus, I've never trusted him. They sly way he comes up to you. It's a wonder to me Mrs Sanderson lets the thing wander about freely like that. I'll speak to her.'

It was a secret. Nobody knew but himself. He wouldn't tell her till he was safely in bed that it wasn't Rastus, it was the merchant's dog, Solomon, that had bitten him. Maybe they would have to cut off his leg. He sat erect in the chair and gave out long quivering sobs.

Mary-Anne took a small round purple bottle from the cupboard and gave it to the mother.

Grand-dad muttered from his chair beside the fire, 'That's nothing, a clean bite. There's worse things than that'll happen to him. Fuss, fuss.'

His father had come in and was leaning against the kitchen doorpost, watching him, and his pipe glowed and faded in the interior gloom.

Great jags of flame went into his thigh. He screamed and held on desperately to his mother. 'It's all right, darling,' she said. 'I'm putting a drop of lysol on. That'll make you better.'

The disinfectant flamed and flickered and guttered in his

white flesh. The faces came about him again. Freda was
smiling – she seemed to be pleased at his sufferings. His father's
pipe glowed and faded and glowed. He was the important
person in the house that day. He sobbed and sniffed in a long
last luxury of self-pity. His mother cut a piece of lint with the
scissors.

4

Colm crouched among the tall grasses of the dune. 'Colm,
where are you? You must come home. . . .' It was Ellen's voice
that went wandering along the sea-banks, here and there,
seeking him out. He wished Ellen would go away. 'Colm,
something has happened. . . .' His grandfather was dead, that's
what had happened. He knew without Ellen having to come
and tell him. The old man had lain ill for ten days in the parlour
bed. A deepening silence had gathered about him. The mother
and children passed from room to room in whispers. He lay
there, a lonely stricken figure. 'Colm, mam wants you home
now. . . .' He pretended not to hear Ellen's quavering command.
He scooped up a handful of sand and let it stream through his
fingers. He left the dune and slipped like a shadow down to the
shore. If Ellen came that way he would hide in the cave. 'Colm,
it's grand-dad. Hurry up. . . .' He wished Ellen would go away
and leave him alone. He did not like people spying on his
feelings. He did not feel anything, anyway, in the face of this
suffering and death, except a kind of blank wonderment. He
dipped one foot in a rockpool. A salt vice gripped his ankle.
The coldness reverberated in his belly, tingled in his ear-lobes
and fingers. He turned. His sister was going back across the
field. Colm was the only person on that mile-long sweep of
beach. The sea pulsed slowly over sea-weed and sand. A wave
smashed the bright calm rockpool.

The boy moved across a narrowing strip of sand. It must be
nearly high tide. He sat down on a rock. What was grand-dad
now, an angel? He stood up and sent a flat stone leaping and

skidding over the highest gleam of the sea. It was full flood. 'There'll be more fun in the house now. We'll be able to sing and shout again.' He neither liked nor disliked his grandfather. Grand-dad was just a part of the house, like the cupboard and the straw chair he sat in. Grand-dad could be very grumpy and ill-natured. Grand-dad sat at the fire all winter putting ships into bottles. People on holiday, tourists, English trout fishers, came and bought them from him. Then grand-dad would be pleased, flattening out the pound notes, folding them, stowing them carefully into his purse. The ships-in-bottles were always the same: a three-masted clipper, a rock with a lighthouse, a blue and white curling plaster sea. Grand-dad had been a sailor when he was young. Then he had come home and gone to the fishing. He was very old now. It was grand-dad's house they were living in – would they be put out of it now that he was dead? Grand-dad had almost drowned one day off Braga Rock when he was coming home from the lobsters and a sudden gale had torn the sea apart. He told the story so often that Colm knew it by heart. This past winter grand-dad had added a few new words: 'Life was sweet then. A pleasant thing it was for the eyes to behold the sun. Anyway, I got ashore. But now I would be glad to be taken....' He had become very remote from them all lately. He smoked his pipe still and spat into a spittoon on the floor. His mother had to clean out the spittoon, a horrible job, long slimy clinging slugs of spittle into the burn – the gushing freshness of the burn bore the old man's juices out to sea. Colm and Ellen had to look about the beach for gulls' feathers to clean the bore of his pipe; if they found good ones grand-dad would open his purse carefully and give them a ha'penny each. He stopped making ships-in-bottles soon after New Year. More and more often he would pause in the arm-chair, his pipe half-way to his mouth, as if he was listening for something. For two whole days his pipe had lain cold on the mantelpiece. 'I won't be a trouble to you much longer,' grand-dad had said to mother. He frowned at Ellen and Colm, as if they were strangers trespassing on his peace. The fishing-boat belonged to him too. Would they have to sell it now? What way could his dad go to the fishing if they had no boat? Maybe they would starve. Colm walked up the cart-track from the beach. He sat down on the grass and put on his sandals. The sea pulsed, a slow diastole of ebb; it surged in still, but left shining fringes; the forsaken sand gleamed dully. They would all have to wear black clothes, or at least black cloth diamonds on the sleeves of their coats and jackets. That was horrible. There would have to be the funeral, of course. His grand-dad would be put deep in the churchyard: frail old bones, silky beard, sunk jaws. The wood of the coffin would begin to rot in the wet winter earth. Then spring would come, but grand-dad would know nothing about it. There were cornfields all about the kirkyard. In summer the land would be athrob with ripeness, the roots in the kirkyard too. Grand-dad would have 'given his flesh to increase the earth's ripeness': that was Jock Skaill the tailor's way of looking at it. That, he assured Colm, was the meaning of death. But most of the Norday women said nobody, least of all a child, should pay attention to an atheist like Jock Skaill. Still, there was more in what Jock Skaill said, in Colm's opinion, than in all that talk about angels and harps and streets of gold. His grand-dad would be lost in a heaven like that. 'My grand-father, Andrew Sinclair the fisherman, is dead.' He could not really believe it. Merran Wylie was flinging oats to her hens at the end of her croft. The boy and the woman looked at each other in passing. Merran shook her head sorrowfully, then emptied her aluminium bowl and went hurriedly back in through her door. When he turned the corner there it was, down at the shore, their house with the blinds drawn against the sweetness of day. The whole house looked blind and bereft. The door opened and a woman who had no right to be there shook his mother's rug and went in again, leaving the door open: Jessie Gray from Garth. All the village women had united to help his mother. That's what happened whenever anybody died. Bella Simison from the Smithy came to the open door and stood looking out over the fields, shading her eyes with her hand. They were all wondering about him, Colm, for of course he should be in the house with the rest of the family at such an important time. He stood behind the fuchsia bush in the manse garden till Mrs Simison had gone in again. It was Saturday. He heard shouts from the end of the village: the boys were playing football in the quarry field. Their shouts sounded profane. They did not understand the gravity of what had happened. Colm felt as if he was about to enter a solemn temple. He heard voices over the high wall of Sunnybrae. 'Yes, so I hear, Andrew Sinclair the fisherman.... About ten this morning. He's well relieved, the poor old man. Two strokes in a week....' The minister's wife and Mrs Spence of Sunnybrae, Captain Spence's widow, were talking about the death of his grand-dad.

He ran swiftly and silently across the grass to the house of death.

He stood with fluttering breath in the open door. The kitchen was full of gray whispers and moving shadows. He exchanged, furtively, the light for the gloom of the lobby.

His mother's face was purified, as if a fire had passed through it. She sat in the straw-back chair beside the dresser. The village women fussed around her. One was making tea at the stove. One was washing the best china in preparation for (probably) the funeral meal. Jessie Gray was telling stories about Andrew Sinclair – all the memorable things he had done and said in his life: from time to time the other women shook their heads slowly and smiled. Mrs Sanderson from Wardings farm was baking bannocks on the girdle. The only grieving creatures in the house were the two younger girls. Freda and Ellen hung about with blubbered faces and large eyes in the darkest corner of the room. His father sat in the window-seat; he looked uncomfortable in the company of all these priestesses of death. Freda and Ellen glanced reproachfully at Colm as he entered, silently, the kitchen.

The village women turned grave complacent faces on the newcomer.

'Colm,' said his mother in a queer artificial voice, 'your grandfather's passed away.'

'I know,' he muttered ill-naturedly.

It was not death. It was a kind of solemn game with words and gestures, a feast of flowers and false memories.

He followed Jessie Gray into the parlour.

Even when he looked down on the strange familiar cold face on the pillow it was still all a mime to give importance and dignity to a poor house. Two of the village women looked smilingly down at the corpse from the other side of the bed. Grand-dad's face was a still pool.

'Touch the brow with your hand.' It was the tranquil voice of Jessie Gray, who knew all about the trappings and ceremonies of death; she had prepared a hundred corpses for the kirkyard in her time.

Colm put two fingers, lightly, to his grandfather's forehead; they winced from an intense and bitter coldness. He could have cried out with terror. Now he knew that his grandfather was dead indeed.

He saw the cold pipe on the bedside table. He remembered the gulls' feathers and the ha'pennies. His grand-dad had been a very sweet kind old man.

The women watched him slyly. He knew these women. They were waiting for him to burst into tears. That was the pious thing for a boy to do. Then they would come about the bereaved one with their false hearty comfortings. He hated to have his feelings spied on. He would not cry to please them.

'How peaceful he looks,' said Jessie Gray.

He looked earnestly into the cold pool that was growing rigid, even while he looked and wondered, with the frost of death.

5

'Alice, tell them what I mean by the phrase "colours of the

spectrum",' said Miss Silver.

Alice Rendall was the cleverest pupil in the Norday school. When the ten-year-olds were arranged in order of merit at the start of each week, Alice sat always at the top seat with the class medal pinned to her jersey: a heavy lead disc with *For Merit* stamped on it. The little ring on top of the medal blossomed with a ribbon.

Colm sometimes had the feeling that Alice was made of china rather than flesh, there was such fragility and coldness and cleanness about her. She did not get into trouble of any kind – did not whisper to her neighbours or pass notes – did not suck pan-drops through her handkerchief – did not leave her coat in school when the sun broke the rain-clouds – had never been known to raise her hand, untimely, with an urgent 'Please, miss, may I leave the room?' Some of the girls were not above showing the fringes of their knickers to the boys under the desk; never Alice. Her face shone each morning from much soap-and-water and a soft towel.

Alice was good at nearly everything: sums, reading, writing, spelling, history, geography. She did not have much of a singing voice, it was true. Her drawings were not as good as Willie Hume's. And she could not run and somersault as well as most of the other girls. 'Alice Rendall, you have the highest marks this week again,' said Miss Silver regularly every Friday afternoon. 'You will sit at the top of the class on Monday morning. Well done, Alice. Second, John Hay. Third, James Marcusson....'

Colm was not particularly good at any subject. He liked history. He was bad at drawing and geography. He did a strange perverse thing every Friday: he deliberately falsified his marks, downgraded himself, so that he could share the bottom place in class with a boy called Phil Kerston. As surely as Alice Rendall was dux each week, Philip Kerston was dunce. Phil was utterly ignorant of every subject on the school curriculum. But he could snare rabbits. He could light fires in a gale. He had taken eggs from the face of Hundhead, the highest cliff in the island.

Miss Silver gave Phil jobs to do, such as look after the school fire in winter, wipe the blackboard clean with a duster, and fill the ink-wells. In school he was good-natured and quiet.

Colm sat beside Phil Kerston whenever he could. The smell of rabbits and grass-fires attracted him. Another part of the attraction was that he was a little afraid of the strange wild ignorant boy.

One Friday afternoon Phil Kerston and Colm whispered together on the front seat while Miss Silver wrote multiplication tables on the blackboard. Tomorrow, Saturday, they were to burn heather among the hills. Colm promised to bring a box of matches. He would buy it with the penny he got every Saturday from his father.

Colm ran through the gap in the hills, breathless, after Phil Kerston and Andrick Overton. The sun was hot on the gray rocks. A bee blundered from heather-bell to heather-bell. Colm stumbled up the cart track.

He stood between the two hills, Brunafea and Torfea, and looked back. Phil and Andrick had gone on ahead, into the heart of the island. Colm had never been as far as this before. He did not like to be too far away from his mother's door. He saw the village down below, and the beach with a few boats hauled up, and small moving toy cows in the field of Wardings.

So, up here was where the farmers and crofters dug their winter fires. The long deep black lines of the peat-banks stretched across a flank of Brunafea that could not be seen from the village.

But he would have to hurry. Phil Kerston and Andrick Overton were two lost voices, thin and sweet, answering each other from the interior of the island. They would not wait for Colm, who couldn't move as fast as them on account of the asthma that bothered him sometimes in the summer. They had taken his box of matches from him and gone on up.

Colm did not like to be alone in strange places. He had got his breath back now. He ran on, between the summer hills, in the direction of the voices.

He rounded a shoulder of Torfea, a little stony outcrop, and a world he had never seen before opened out before him: the barren interior of Norday. He caught his breath, it was so lonely and beautiful. There was not a croft in sight. There was nothing but sweeps of moor and bog, and, like a jewel among the starkness, a little loch. A hidden burn sang under Colm's feet. A lark, very high up, drenched the desolation with song.

Colm ran down towards the loch that was still half-a-mile away. It was Tumilshun Loch. He had heard his father and the other men speaking about it in the smithy. He had seen the English trout-fishers in summer setting out with rod and reel for the place. These men with the loud voices and thick tweeds would bide among the hills still sunset. A small shiver went over Colm's skin. He would not care to spend even an hour in such a desolate place.

Where were Phil and Andrick? He couldn't hear them any more. They might be gathering blackberries. Andrick had brought a tin can for that purpose. Colm went down a few paces more in the direction of the loch. A sprig of heather scratched his bare ankle. He put his hand to his mouth. 'Phil,' he called out, 'where are you?'

The shadow of a cloud moved across Brunafea.

It was unnerving, the sound of his voice. It was like blasphemy. It bounced off the craggy face of Brunafea. It seemed to shiver across the face of the loch. It came back to him, all eeriness and mockery, and died among the far hills. Colm listened, appalled. His heart pounded in his chest.

Why didn't Phil and Andrick answer him? He would not shout like that again.

It was then that the hinterland was drained suddenly of all its colour. The lark stopped singing. The sun had gone behind a cloud.

Tumilshun lay there below, a sheet of dead pewter. Colm remembered how his father had told him that it was a very deep loch: in his time two people had committed suicide in it. Fifty years ago a girl from the croft of Swenquoy was found floating among the reeds.

Colm faced quickly back towards the gap in the hills. He climbed like a goat, from rock to heather-clump, out of the awful landscape. He could not have uttered another cry – terror had numbed his throat. He fell and rose and fell among the clumps of heather. A flood of light came over the flank of Torfea and enveloped him. He ran on. Only when he could see a segment of ocean between the hills did he turn back: there Tumilshun lay, a dark blue gleam, far below him. And there, between the loch and the lower slope of Brunafea, was a red-gray smudge. Phil and Andrick had lit their fires, and gone on.

The lark, empty of song, eased itself down. It guttered out among the coarse grass.

With a surge of joy (but ashamed at the same time of his cowardice) Colm emerged from the sinister region and saw below him the squares of tilth and pasture, and the village; and Tom of Wardings cutting hay in his field with a flashing scythe. Further away, between the ness and the holm, the *Godspeed* entered the bay.

'Poetry,' said Miss Silver. 'William Wordsworth. "Fidelity". Page 35 in your books.'

Colm bent his head over the page. He read, silently.

> A barking sound the shepherd hears,
> A cry as of a dog or fox.
> He halts – and searches with his eyes
> Among the scattered rocks:
> And now at distance can discern
> A stirring in a brake of fern;

And instantly a dog is seen
Glancing through that covert green.

'You will learn this verse for recitation tomorrow morning,'
said Miss Silver to the ten-year-olds.

Poetry was hated by the whole school. The children's natural
style of recitation, a chant heavily accented, was condemned by
Miss Silver (who had been taught Elocution at her teachers'
training college). 'No,' she said, 'You mustn't drone on mono-
tonously like that. You must recite the poem with *expression*.
Like this. Listen.

A *barking* sound the SHEPHERD hears,
A CRY as of a *dog* or *fox*. . . .'

The only poetry the island children knew were the surrealist
word-games – corn-spells, fish-spells, ancestral memories of
murder and grief and illicit love made innocent and lyrical –
that they played in the school playground.

Water water wallflower
Growing up so high
We are all maidens
And we must all die. . . .

None of the island children could recite 'with expression';
Alice Rendall could, a little. So they disliked poetry, especially
when they were given verses to learn by rote for Tuesday afternoon, which was the time devoted to poetry and recitation.
Every Monday evening, therefore, in a dozen scattered crofts,
the same ritual took place: at the kitchen table, under the
paraffin lamp, innocent mouths moved silently and resentfully
above the school poetry book, again and again; until their own
sweet natural rhythms were crushed under the relentless stone.

There sometimes doth a leaping fish
Send through the tarn a lonely cheer;
The crags repeat the raven's croak

> In symphony austere.
> Thither the rainbow comes – the cloud –
> And mists that spread the flying shroud;
> And sunbeams; and the sounding blast,
> That, if it could, would hurry past;
> But that enormous barrier holds it fast.

Colm read the verse idly, once, before bed-time. The book lay open on the scrubbed table. *A lonely cheer.* His breath trembled on his lip. He subjected the page to a silent absorbed scrutiny. It was a lonely experience, like death or nakedness. His mouth moulded the words: *mists that spread the flying shroud.* He hoarded the lines, phrase by phrase.

It was the interior of Norday that was being bodied forth in a few words.

The lamp splashed the page with yellow light.

This poet must have seen Tumilshun too, or else some loch very like it. He had felt the same things as Colm. This was strange, that somebody else (and him a famous dead poet) felt the dread, for none of the other boys seemed to; at least, if they did, they never spoke about it. But this was even stranger: there was a joy at the heart of the desolation. Colm could not explain it. It was as if the loch had a secret existence of its own. The hills stood about the loch, silent presences; they were frightening too, when you were among them, but the boy had an obscure feeling that his flesh was made of the same dust as the hills. They bore with ageless patience the scars of the peat-cutters on their shoulders. Colm felt a kinship with that high austere landscape, a first fugitive love.

The poem had worked the change.

His lips moulded, again, the incantation.

> There sometimes doth a leaping fish
> Send through the tarn a lonely cheer....

'Colm, it's long past your bed-time,' said his mother. 'Your face is white as chalk. Close that book now....'

Colm stood at his desk next afternoon, when his turn to recite came. He uttered the magical words in a high nervous treble. He looked down sideways at Phil Kerston. Phil Kerston had taken trout out of Tumilshun with his hands; his father's croft was thatched with heather from the flank of Brunafea; Phil was bound to like the poem, far more even than he did himself. But Phil sat knotting a piece of wire under his desk, idly, making a rabbit snare. Poetry to him was just another cell in the dark prison of school.

'De-dum-de-dum-de-dum,' said Miss Silver. 'No, Colm. You have learned the words, good, but you destroy the life of the poem the way you recite it. Listen now. This is the way it should be spoken: "There sometimes doth a *leaping* FISH...."'

One day that same term Miss Silver said to the ten-year-olds, 'We have all learned at last to read, fairly fluently, out of our school text books, have we not? All except Philip Kerston, but Philip may learn to read in time. Don't worry, Philip. There is something equally important – writing. You must learn how to express yourselves on paper. For, when you leave school, there will be letters to write. Now, won't there, Willie? You don't know? Of course there will.... Perhaps one or two of you will be sailors far away from home, so you will want your parents to know how you are getting on, in Sydney, or Port Said, or Bombay perhaps. Even those who stay in the island will also need to know how to express themselves. For, perhaps Maisie Smith will be made secretary of the W.R.I. – no laughter, please – or Stephen Will of the Agricultural Society, and then Maisie or Stephen will be expected to make up minutes of the proceedings and also send a report to *The Orcadian*.... Learning to write correctly is called what, Alice?'

'Composition,' said Alice Rendall.

'It is called composition,' said Miss Silver. 'We are going to write our very first composition this morning. Philip, fill the ink-pots that are empty or nearly empty. John Hay, pass round those new composition exercise books. The compositions are to be written in ink. I want your very best writing, remember. Does everyone have a blotter? Very well, then. Listen. The subject of the composition is this: "The World I see from my Door".'

A dozen pens scratched and hesitated across white pages for an hour.

Colm wrote idly to begin with, about the lupins in his mother's garden. They grew in summer between the rhubarb and the potato patch. If he stood on the low wall he could see the beach, his father's boat, the sea. Some days, after a westerly gale, Corporal Hourston would come to the shore looking for jetsam. The corporal was a beachcomber. One winter night he stood in the door and there were stars in the sky, hundreds of them, and a full moon. Snow had fallen all day. The furrows in a field at Wardings were long purple shadows. Some days he stood in the door watching for his father's boat to come back from the fishing. He was uneasy whenever *Godspeed* was late. Then everything he saw looked gray, the sea and the sky. The thoughts that went through his mind seemed to be gray too. One day he was alone in the house and he heard a knock at the door. He opened it. He saw a tinker wife standing there with a stumpy pipe in her mouth and a pack on her back. . . .

Colm did not suppose he would be better at composition than he was at arithmetic or geography. He discovered that he could remember things much better writing them down than speaking them. When he had time to assemble his material the past ceased to be a confused flux; it became a sequence of images, one image growing out of another and contrasting with it, and anticipating too the inevitable exciting image that must follow. He liked making sentences. He put commas in, and full stops; in that way he could make the word sequences (which were, of course, inseparable from the image sequences) flow fast or slow; whichever seemed more suitable. He even put a semi-colon in the part about the moon and the snow, and then the sentence seemed to hang balanced like a wind-slewed gull. Writing gave Colm a small comfortable sense of power.

'Time up,' called Miss Silver. 'Blot the page carefully. Philip Kerston, gather the composition books and bring them to my desk.'

Next morning Miss Silver handed the corrected compositions back.

Alice Rendall sat, demure and erect, at the top of the class.

'You have a great deal to learn, all of you,' said Miss Silver, 'about how to write English properly. Spelling and punctuation were, on the whole, dreadful. On the other hand, some efforts were quite promising. Alice wrote a nice composition about the hill of Torfea, with its wild birds, its muirburn, its peat-cutters, etcetera. You can see all that from the door of your father's farm, can't you, Alice? However, the best composition of all was written by Colm Sinclair. Well done, Colm. Colm, I want you to come out to the floor and read your composition to the school. Listen, everybody. It is really quite original and good.'

He stood beside Miss Silver's desk, his composition book in his hand, trying to control his nervous breaths. He read: "The door of our house is made out of an oak beam that my great-grandfather found a hundred years ago at the beach under Hundhead...."

Then the school heard another new sound. A score of faces looked round, startled. It was Alice. Her head was down on the desk; her little fists trembled; spasm after spasm went through her body. The girl was sobbing as if her heart would break.

6

After tea one Saturday night, it rained. Colm put on his coat and cap and went to the tailor shop at the end of the village.

Jock Skaill the tailor was his best friend in Norday, though he was forty years older than Colm. The islanders could never make up their minds about Jock Skaill: the women were always gossiping about him in the store. – *Jock Skaill says there's no God. . . . He's a communist. . . . They say he has bairns somewhere in the south. . . . Him and his drink. . . . They say he was in prison for a while. . . . He was the death of that wife of his, if you ask me. . . .* The bitter mouths. The head-shakings. The shuttered brows.

Colm's mother wouldn't have it. She maintained always that Jock Skaill was a fine man. She knew him; they had attended school together; they had been neighbours in the village when they were children.

'Jock Skaill,' she would say, 'he's had an unfortunate life, if you think about it. He was the cleverest boy by far in Norday School, he could have gone on to the university and everything. But old Tom his father would have no grandiose nonsense of that kind. When Jock left school he had to go and sit at that tailor's bench. He hated it – you could see that he was like a young dog tied up in a shed. So when old Tom died he just put up the shutters and left the island without a word to anybody. I suppose he went to sea. What if he did have a wild year or two of it? It's a queer chap that doesn't sow his wild oats in his twenties. There's many a good man been in jail – John Bunyan for example, and James Maxton, and Gandhi. Well, he came home and opened the shop again and he married that girl from Hamnavoe, Susan Fea, and I'm sure no couple were ever happier than them for a year or two. And then the poor lass, she went into some kind of a decline, you know, consumption, and she died in the sanatorium in Kirkwall. Between one thing and another Jock Skaill's had a stony path to tread. It hasn't soured him at all, that's the wonder. He's the kindest cheerfulest man in this island. . . .'

Thus his mother on Jock Skaill the island tailor, whenever the subject was raised with malicious intent in her presence.

But Jessie Gray and Bella Simison would turn down their

mouths and keep on muttering about communists and atheists and jailbirds....

Colm hung his damp coat on a nail in the door. Jock Skaill cleared bits of cloth, shears, a tiny triangle of chalk, a few books, the cat's milk saucer, from the end of the bench. He set out the draught-board. He put a few peats into the stove.

They played silently that night, two dreaming faces over the bench in the lamplight. It was a leisurely dance and counter-dance of pieces across the board. Outside the rain drummed on the dingy window-panes.

Jock Skaill only spoke when a game was over and he was filling his pipe, and Colm was arranging the counters on the board once more.

'Four years next Wednesday since Susan died. Susan was my wife. "There is a happy land far far away...." Don't you believe it, boy. She came out of the earth and we were happy for two years and three months, and then she went back to the earth. That's the way I think of her. She's a part of the rich beautiful earth....There's the cat scratching on the door. Let him in out of the rain.'

Colm won the first game.

'It's a grand feeling, to know you have children. Get married, boy, have children, but not too many – the world's full enough as it is. I have a child that I've never seen. Withered folk, grandparents, they came between the boy's mother and me. I had a great liking for that girl. I'm glad that somewhere in England there's a piece of me, a living body that came out of my own body. He walks in the wind and the sun. He will make a new human being when the time comes. That's the only kind of immortality there is....That fire needs a few peats.'

Jock Skaill won the second game.

'The gossiping old women, I don't mind them at all. They've been at it since the world was young. The Greek choruses began with the likes of Jessie Gray and Bella Simison. What grieves me is the change that's come over the men in this island.

They used to tell stories, not the old women's title-tattle, but the legends of the island, what their great-grandfathers said and did. That's the source of all poetry and drama. Not now – they discuss what they read in the newspapers and hear on their wireless sets, they have opinions about Free Trade and the Irish Question. I swear to God it makes me laugh to hear them going on about Ramsay Macdonald and Life on Mars, down there in the smithy. All so knowledgeable and important, and not one original idea among them. The marvellous old legends, that's beneath them now. . . . I'm boring you, I expect. If you open that drawer you'll find a poke of butternuts.'

Jock won the third game also.

'Progress, that's the modern curse. This island is enchanted with the idea of Progress. Look at what we have now – reapers, wireless sets, free education, motor bikes, white bread. Times are much easier for us than for our grandfathers. So, they argue, we have better fuller richer lives. It is a God-damned lie. This worship of Progress, it will drain the life out of every island and lonely place. In three generations Norday will be empty. For, says Progress, life in a city *must* be superior to life in an island. Also, Progress says, "Here is a combine harvester, it will do the work of a score of peasants. . . ." Down we go on our knees again in wonderment and gratitude. . . . Will there be a few folk left in the world, when Progress is choked at last in its own too much? Yes, there will be. A few folk will return by stealth to the wind and the mist and the silences. I know it. . . . Would you reach up for the tea caddy – the kettle's boiling.'

Jock won the fourth game also and so there was no need to play a decider.

They drank tea out of rather filthy mugs, after the draught-board was folded and put away. Then Jock Skaill told him about some of the old men in Norday that he remembered, and some of the shipmates he had sailed with.

Then he said, 'You better be getting home now, boy.

Tomorrow's Sunday. Tell your mother I'm asking for her. Go home. They'll be saying in the store on Monday morning that I'm a corruption to you, if they aren't saying it already.'

7

His mother said, 'Colm, go and see if you can find your father. He's in the shed, most likely.' Torquil and Ellen were spreading butter on their oatcakes. Supper had begun without a blessing from the head of the house.

The shed on the pier was a black unlighted cube.

Colm wandered up the shore road to the village. His father was most likely in the smithy. A few of the village men gathered in Steve Simison's smithy in the dark evenings. What would they be talking about tonight? The last time Colm had been in the smithy they had been discussing The Yellow Peril.

He entered the smithy shyly. A paraffin lamp hung from the rafters. There were a few men sitting round the anvil. Steve Simison had taken off his leather apron and washed his face and hands; he had a white pure look about him. There indeed was his father, sitting on the bench.

The black maw of the forge gave out a warmth still.

None of the men let on to notice the boy.

Colm tried to catch his father's eye but the company was deep in some discussion: grave tilted faces under the lamp, furrowed brows.

Colm listened. They were talking about the date of Easter.

'I can't understand it,' said Mr William Smith the general merchant. (He was probably the most important man in the island, now that the laird had declined into genteel poverty. He kept the shop in the village and his merchandise comprised everything: groceries, wine, bread and cakes, footwear, butcher-meat, confectionary, fruit, flowers and wreaths, draperies. In addition he was the county councillor for the island, and vice-president of the local Liberal Party, and session clerk, and registrar, and Justice of the Peace. Everyone heard him always with the greatest respect.)

'I can't for the life of me understand it,' he was saying. 'It shifts about from year to year. *I'll be wanting the usual lilies and daffodils for Easter – would you order them please?* says Miss Siegfried in the shop a fortnight ago. So, thinks I to myself, there's plenty of time. In she comes again this morning. *I'll take the flowers now*, says she, *if they've come*. I had been meaning to write all week to the florist in Kirkwall. *I think we should wait till nearer the time*, says I. *Then they'll be fresh*....She looks at me like the far end of a fiddle. *Tomorrow's Good Friday*, she says. *This is Maundy Thursday. I require the flowers for the chapel on Easter morning. I'm afraid it might be too late now.*'

'Easter was a lot later indeed last year,' said Dod Sabiston, 'if I'm not mistaken.'

'*This is Maundy Thursday*,' said William Smith, imitating quite well the loud posh English accent of Miss Siegfried the laird's sister. 'Of course they're Episcopalians up at The Hall. So there I was in a fine fix, I can tell you.'

'But why should it be?' said Colm's father, Timothy Sinclair the fisherman. 'Why should Easter be one date this year and another date next year? I could never fathom that.'

Colm stood there silently, his eyes going from face to face.

'God knows,' said the blacksmith. 'Christmas now, that's the same date every year.'

There was silence for half a minute. Then Corporal Hourston cleared his throat and combed with his fingers his handsome moustache: a sign that he had something to say. Corporal Hourston was a retired soldier, and lived on a small pension at the end of the village, in a poor hovel of a place. He had gathered hundreds of bits of useless wisdom from Egypt, Hindustan, the Transvaal. The village men deferred to him. half mocking, half respectful.

'It's the Pope that decides,' said Corporal Hourston sententiously. 'The Pope decides the date of Easter every year for the whole world.'

They pondered this, gravely.

'The Pope,' said Mr Smith, offended. 'The Pope. The Pope has no authority over *us*.'

'No, we're Presbyterians,' said Timothy Sinclair. 'We threw off that yoke a long time ago.'

'The Pope indeed!' said Mr Smith. He turned to Colm's father. 'You're right, Tim,' he said. 'That was the Reformation. And it didn't happen a moment too soon, if you ask me.'

'It was Martin Luther that saved us from the Pope,' said Dod Sabiston of Dale.

'No,' said Andrew Custer the saddler, who was also a deacon in the kirk, 'it wasn't Martin Luther. The English Protestants followed Martin Luther. The Presbyterians followed John Calvin. Luther was a German.'

They nodded, sagely.

'It's very hard to credit,' said Mr Smith, 'that people could ever be taken in by such darkness.'

'We were all Roman Catholics once,' said Corporal Hourston. 'All our forefathers here in Orkney were Roman Catholics.'

'That was a long time ago,' said Timothy Sinclair. 'People were very ignorant in those days. There was no education. They couldn't read the Bible. They knew no better. They had to believe whatever the priests told them to believe.'

'The Pope, though, he still rules a great part of the world,' said Andrew Custer. 'France, Italy, Spain, South America.'

'And Ireland too,' said Corporal Hourston.

'The Irish people are very poor,' said Mr Smith. 'Very poor and very oppressed. You'll find, if you study the matter, that all Roman Catholic countries are very backward.'

The forge was sending out lessening circles of warmth. Colm shivered a little. He moved nearer to the wise deliberate lit mouths. He was glad that he did not live in Ireland or Spain. He was pleased too that his father had a respected word in these smithy counsels. His father had thought about things and formed his own opinions. He was only a fisherman but the other men listened gravely whenever Timothy Sinclair opened his mouth. There was a stack of books in their house, in the window shelf. His father read for a long time every night in winter after the young ones were in bed. *The Rat Pit* by Patrick MacGill. *My school and Schoolmasters* by Hugh Miller. *People of the Abyss* by Jack London. *Now Barabbas* by Marie Corelli. *Selected Poems and Letters of Robert Burns.* These were only a few of the titles on the window shelf. His father was well respected in Norday for his earnestness and literacy. He was another one who could have 'gotten on' if poverty hadn't kept him tied to his fishing boat.

'You would hardly credit it,' said Andrew Custer, 'but they worship the Virgin Mary.'

A new face appeared from behind the forge. Mrs Bella Simison stood there. She had come no doubt on the same errand as Colm, to get the breadwinner in to his supper. But she saw the ring of contemptuous slightly shocked faces, and stood listening.

'When I have sinned,' said Mr Smith, 'I ask for God's forgiveness. We all sin, we are frail mortal clay, the best of us. But your Catholic, he goes to a priest to be forgiven, he tells his sins to a man who is a sinner like himself.'

'That's not all, William,' said Dod Sabiston. 'He has to give the priest money to forgive him.'

Timothy Sinclair and Steve Simison shook their heads incredulously. Only Corporal Hourston seemed unmoved: he had known worse things beside the Brahmaputra – sacred hens, crocodiles, cows, widows and infants laid alive on burning pyres.

'That there should be such darkness in the human mind,' said Mr Smith. 'When I want to talk to my Maker, I pray. I tell him how things are with me. I ask for guidance. Your Roman Catholic takes out his rosary beads. He counts them over and over. He mumbles the "vain repetitions" that we are warned against in scripture.'

The Virgin Mary. Priests in black, accepting money from sinners. Rosary beads. Colm shivered with supernatural dread. The dark pool of the human mind. He moved closer in to the fading warmth of the forge.

'Then they die,' said Mr Smith. 'But they do not go like you and me to glory or the bad place, according as we have lived our mortal lives. O no, they go to Purgatory, a place that as far as I know is nowhere mentioned in scripture.'

'No, William,' said Andrew Custer, 'but money comes into that too. You pay to get your friends out of Purgatory. The more you pay, the sooner they get out. That's what they believe.'

Purgatory: another word to add to his sinister hoard.

Corporal Hourston cleared his throat. 'I fought beside Irishmen at Ladysmith,' he said. 'They were all Roman Catholics. They were very good soldiers. Lord Lovat was the commander-in-chief. If I'm not mistaken Lord Lovat was a Roman Catholic too, but of course he was a Scotsman.'

'I once went into a Roman Catholic kirk in Glasgow,' said Dod Sabiston. 'It was full of statues that they prayed to. There was this old woman lighting candles in front of a plaster saint. Graven images everywhere. And the smell of incense, I'm telling you, it was enough to make a man's stomach heave.'

Colm noticed a face that he had not seen at first when he came into the smithy. Tom Sanderson of Wardings had been sitting silent all the time in a dark corner that was studded with old rusty horse-shoes. He was smiling quietly to himself. He took his pipe out of his mouth. He looked over at Colm and shook his head gently and smiled.

Bella Simison spoke up from beside the forge in her deep rapid stacatto. 'Don't tell me about Catholics, them and their carry-on, I have a book in the house, Tina Wasbister took it from Edinburgh, *Maria Monk*, that's the name on it, about nuns in a convent, O my God what a carry-on, them and the priests, supposed never to marry, and babies born every now and then, first done away with, then buried, the poor innocent things, in quick-lime. Well, this Maria Monk, she was a nun too, and she tried to get out and . . . .'

'That's all right,' said Steve Simison coldly to his wife. 'I'm just closing up. Then I'll be in for my supper.'

'You can't tell me anything I don't know about Roman Catholics,' cried Bella. She turned her flushed face from one to the other. 'I'll give you the book to read, anybody that wants it, a loan of.' Then she withdrew, in the darkness, to the smell of kippers that came from the open door beyond the forge.

One by one the men got to their feet. Colm's father lowered himself from the bench. Steve Simison closed the forge and put on his jacket. It was beginning to be very cold in the smithy.

'No doubt but it is a great abomination,' said Anthrew Custer solemnly. 'It is The Scarlet Woman spoken of in the Bible. It is the Whore of Babylon. It is the abomination of desolation.'

Steve Simison raised the lamp glass and blew out the flame.

They moved one after the other towards the door, feeling their ways.

'I'll tell you a very strange thing,' said Mr Smith. 'When I was a boy the gravedigger was old Thomas Wylie. None of you will mind him. Well, Thomas, he was called on to dig a grave in the oldest part of the cemetery, you know, beside the ruined wall where there are no stones at all, only a shallow hump here and there. That's where the people were buried when Orkney was a Catholic place. Well, when old Thomas was digging the grave he came on a hoard of silver and gold coins. The story was told often when I was a boy. I marvelled at that and I still do – burying money with a corpse.'

They stood together on the dark road outside the smithy. Corporal Hourston clicked his heels and, grave and erect, marched off in the direction of his cottage. Steve Simison closed the smithy door and barred it from the inside. Colm put his cold hand into his father's great warm rough hand. There were squares of light here and there in the darkling village.

'What I can't understand,' said Mr Smith, 'is why they can't grow their own daffodils and lilies. They have a big enough garden, God knows, up there at The Hall, and it's all choked with weeds!'...He gave his imitation of Miss Siegfried's cut-glass accent, '*I assure you, Mr Smith, tomorrow is Good Friday, and I require the flowers for the chapel on Sunday, and you promised, you know, you promised.*'

Dark fragments of laughter, and 'goodnights'. Colm walked with his father to their house: to the fire, the table with its milk and oatcakes, the bed where he would soon kneel and say his one simple good Presbyterian prayer.

8

The young man, because of asthma, had hardly slept all night. His breathing was always more laboured in the city in the middle of summer. There had been three or four warm July days – hot days even, for Edinburgh. The canyon of the street where he lodged kept still, after midnight, some of its gathered warmth. It brimmed through the high dark window of his bed-sitter. He sweated under his single blanket, and longed for morning.

He must have drowsed for an hour or so; when he looked again the window was a silver-gray square. There would be dawn over the North Sea now, trying to burn its way through the early mists.

The man had done no work on his novel since the start of the golden weather. The sun from morning to night, among the city streets, even across the handsome squares and gardens, distracted him. His imagination was dislocated. Writing became a burden not to be borne. For the past two days he had taken a bus out to the village of Cramond on the Firth of Forth, thinking that the sea might help him. He had sat on the rocks, smoking, and watched the picnics, the children bathing, the sailing boats. But even here there was no release: he felt his loneliness like a pain. He envied the happy young folk with their towels and bottles of coke. Yesterday he had gone to

Cramond again, but he had spent most of the day in the Inn, drinking iced lager.

He wished, this cold northern man, that the sun would stop shining, so that he could put his loneliness to some use, and get his writing done. He wished, alternatively, that he could pack his bag and settle with Mrs Doyle his landlady and take a boat north. And the longing and the loneliness ground out between them this asthma that distressed his daytime and kept him awake half the night.

The window brightened, quite suddenly. The sun, hidden by the tall tenements of Marchmont, had ruptured the sea haar. It was going to be another breathless idle day for him. He looked at his watch; it was passing five o'clock. He decided to get up and, before the day made him inert, write a letter.

'Dear Jock – I am not coming north this year. There are it's true so many things I want to see – Tumilshun and the hills, the churchyard, the school, the piers where I fished and the ditches where I burned my fingers. But there are other places that give me a pain at the heart when I think of them – the doorless houses in the village, the *Godspeed* rotting on the beach, the black forge, the mill with its great stones dusty and silent.

'I can only finish this new novel in a cold neutral unhaunted place.

'Thank you for that last letter. That you liked *The Rock Pastures* gives me more genuine pleasure than if, for example, Dr Leavis or Professor Trilling had signified their approval. "It tastes of earth and salt. The folk in cities will be none the worse of that", you say. "That is the good thing about all you write. That is your best gift to the world. Even old Tom Sanderson liked it. He told me so, between laughter and head-shakings, when he was here the other day about his new Sabbath suit...."

'Then all those thunderings at the end of the page, against the "idolatry" and the "superstition" that spoil everything! "I will never never understand" you write, "why you have been enchanted by that mumbo-jumbo to such an extent. Giving up old Calvin and his works, that was well done, but you have opened your door to seven devils worse than the first. When you come to Norday in August, in time for the agricultural show – if there is to be one this year, that's to say, for not a month passes but another farmer leaves the island – you must tell me what made you do it. . . ."

'I will try to tell you now, in writing, for I have as you know a heavy awkward peasant tongue. You always beat me in an argument. If I *have* to argue, all I can offer is an unfolding sequence of images: stations that lead to a stone, and silence, and perhaps after that (if I'm lucky) a meaning. Where can I make a start? It isn't too easy, trying to assemble your thoughts at half past five in the morning in a cold Edinburgh bedroom, with the prospect of another day of hurt breathing.

'Who better to begin with – since you mention him – than old Tom Sanderson of Wardings in Norday?

'Tom Sanderson is a simple self-effacing man. In this evil time, indeed, he is ashamed of his coarseness and earthiness when he compared himself with such folk as grocers and clerks and insurance-men. He is, after all, bound upon the same monotonous wheel year after year. There is nothing alluring about the work he does. He wrestles with mud and dung to win a few crusts and flagons from the earth.

'Yet see this peasant for what he is. He stands at the very heart of our civilization. We could conceivably do without soldiers, administrators, engineers, doctors, poets, but we cannot do without that humble earth-worker who breaks the clods each spring. He is the red son of Adam. He represents us all. He it was who left the caves and, lured on by a new vision, made a first clearing in the forest. There he began the ceremony of bread. He ploughed. He sowed seed. He brooded all the suntime upon the braird, the shoot, the ear, the full corn in the ear. He cut that ripeness. He gathered it into a barn. He put upon it flail and millstone and fire, until at last his goodwife set a loaf and an ale-cup on his table.

'He exists in a marvellous ordering of sun and dust and flesh. I can hear Mr Smith the merchant saying, "Nonsense – it's simply that man has learned how to harness the brute blind forces of nature...." I can hear, among the cloth clippings and shears of Norday, a wiser explanation, "Man and nature learned at last to live kindly and helpfully with one another...." But that for me is simply not good enough; it leaves too much out, it doesn't take account of the terror and the exaltation that came upon the first farmer who broke the earth. It was a terrible thing he had done, to put wounds on the great dark mother. But his recklessness and impiety paid off at the end of summer when he stood among the sheaves. Soon there were loaves on his table; he kept every tenth loaf back – the set-apart secret bread. Why? Because he sensed that there was another actor in the cosmic drama, apart from himself and the wounded earth mother: the Wisdom that in the first place had lured him on to shrug off his brutishness – the quickener, ordainer, ripener, orderer, utterer – the peasant with his liking for simplicity called it God. Man made God a gift in exchange for the gifts of life, imagination, and food. But still the primitive guilts and terrors remained, for the fruitful generous earth would have to be wounded with the plough each springtime.

'In the end, to reconcile the divine and the brutish in men, that Wisdom took on itself to endure all that the earth-born endure, birth and hunger and death.

'You have read and digested all those Thinker's Library books on your mantelpiece – Robertson, Ingersoll, Reade – and so you know that no such person as Jesus Christ ever walked the earth; or if indeed some carpenter at the time of Tiberius Caesar left his work-bench to do some preaching in the hills, that doesn't mean that he was an incarnation of God – that was the fruit of a later conspiracy of priests and potentates, to keep the poor in thrall.

'But I believe it. I have for my share of the earth-wisdom

a patch of imagination that I must cultivate to the best of my skill. And my imagination tells me that it is probably so, for the reason that the incarnation is so beautiful. For all artists beauty must be truth: that for them is the sole criterion (and Keats said it 150 years ago). God indeed wept, a child, on the breast of a woman. He spoke to the doctors of law in the temple, to a few faithful bewildered fishermen, to tax-men and soldiers and cripples and prostitutes, to Pilate, even to those who came to glut themselves on his death-pangs. With a *consummatum est* he died. I believe too that he came up out of the grave the way a cornstalk soars into wind and sun from a ruined cell. After a time he returned with his five wounds back into his kingdom. I believe that a desert and a seashore and a lake heard for a few years the sweet thrilling music of the Incarnate Word. What is intriguing is how often the god-man put agricultural images before those fishermen of his: "A sower went forth to sow...." "First the blade, then the ear, after that the full corn in the ear...." "The fields are white towards harvest...." "I am the bread of life...." No writer of genius, Dante or Shakespeare or Tolstoy, could have imagined the recorded utterances of Christ. What a lovely lyric that is about the lilies-of-the-field and Solomon's garments. I'm telling you this as a writer of stories: there's no story I know of so perfectly shaped and phrased as The Prodigal Son or The Good Samaritan. There is nothing in literature so terrible and moving as the Passion of Christ – the imagination of man doesn't reach so far – it *must* have been so. The most awesome and marvellous proof for me is the way he chose to go on nourishing his people after his ascension, in the form of bread. So the brutish life of man is continually possessed, broken, transfigured by the majesty of God.

'What is old Tom of Wardings that his labour should be seen at last to be so precious? Goldsmith and jeweller work with shadows in comparison.

'It is ceremony that makes bearable for us the terrors and

ecstasies that lie deep in the earth and in our earth-nourished human nature. Only the saints can encounter those "realities". What saves us is ceremony. By means of ceremony we keep our foothold in the estate of man, and remain good citizens of the kingdom of the ear of corn. Ceremony makes everything bearable and beautiful for us. Transfigured by ceremony, the truths we could not otherwise endure come to us. We invite them to enter. We set them down at our tables. These angels bring gifts for the house of the soul. . . .

'It is this saving ceremony that you call "idolatry" and "mumbo-jumbo".

'Here, in a storm of mysticism, I end my homily for today.

'I will come back to the island sometime, but this year I must bide in Edinburgh, alone and palely loitering. I promise I will come when this novel is finished. I long to walk by the shore and among the fields, under those cold surging skies. If it rains, I will come and sit on a cloth-strewn bench and listen to monologues about the essential virtue of man, wild flowers, the things that were said and done in Norday before my time. We will perhaps broach a bottle of Orkney whisky. I think I will be content with that.

'I belong to the island. It grieves me to think I should ever be an exile. My flesh is Brunafea. The water of Tumilshun flows in my veins.

'To return for one last time to "idolatry". When first the subject troubled me I read book after book, for and against, and heard great argument about it and about, and got myself into a worse fankle than ever. I might still be lost in those drifts if, in the end, a few random pieces of verse and song – those ceremonies of words – had not touched me to the heart's core:

La sua voluntate e nostra pace. . . .

Withinne the cloistre blisful of thy sydis
Took mannes shap the eterneel love and pees. . . .

I want a black boy to announce to the gold-mined whites
The arrival of the reign of the ear of corn. . . .

Thou mastering me
God! giver of breath and bread;
World's strand, sway of the sea;
Lord of living and dead. . . .

You must sit down, says Love, and taste my meat.
So I did sit and eat. . . .

Moder and maiden
Was never non but she:
Well may swich a lady
Godes moder be. . . .'

Seeing that it would still be another hour before Mrs Catrian Doyle shouted the length of the corridor that the ham-and-eggs was dished, Colm laid his letter to Jock Skaill in his table drawer. He splashed his face in cold water in the bathroom. He put on his jacket and descended the tenement stair.

The chimney tops on the opposite side of the street were smitten with the morning sun. It lay across the Meadows. It emptied itself, a silent golden flood, into the city that was already beginning to clang and chink with dust-bins and milk bottles.

In a beautiful square a quarter of a mile from his lodgings Colm entered a church that from the outside looked like an ordinary Georgian house. Upstairs there were a few elderly women kneeling here and there. The celebrant entered. Colm had not seen this particular priest before – he looked like an Indo-Chinese. Once again, for the thousandth time, Colm watched the ancient endless beautiful ceremony, the exchange of gifts between earth and heaven, dust and spirit, man and God. The transfigured Bread shone momentarily in the saffron fingers of the celebrant. Colm did not take communion. He had a dread of receiving the Sacrament unworthily, and he considered that the envy and self-pity he had indulged in these last few sun-smitten days were blemishes he would have to be purged of.

During the Last Gospel it came to him that in fact it would be the easiest thing in the world for him to go home. There was nothing to keep him here. There were still meaningful patterns to be discerned in the decays of time. The hills of Norday were astir all summer, still, with love, birth, death, resurrection.

The shops were opening when Colm walked back through Marchmont. Awnings were going up on the bright side of the street. Mr Jack the tobacconist stood in his shop door and waved to him. Colm waved back.

'Been to Mass, is it?' said Mrs Doyle. 'Well now, if it isn't the good religious lodger I have staying with me. The bacon got burnt.'

Colm told Mrs Doyle that he would be taking the boat from Leith northwards that afternoon at five o'clock. He would be away from Edinburgh, he thought, for three weeks at least. He would try to be back for the opening of his new play at the Festival. If Mrs Doyle would be good enough to keep his room open for him. . . .

Back in his room, he tore up the letter that he had written that morning. He packed a few shirts and books. His breathing was much easier, now that the decision had been made.

BIOGRAPHICAL NOTE

George Mackay Brown was born in Stromness, where he now lives, in 1921. He read English at Edinburgh University and did postgraduate work on Gerard Manley Hopkins. In 1965 he was awarded an Arts Council Grant for poetry, in 1968 the Society of Authors' Travel Award, in 1969 the Scottish Arts Council Literature Prize, and in 1971 the Katherine Mansfield Short Story Prize. In 1974 he was made an O.B.E. and in 1976 he received an honorary degree from the Open University. His work has been published in Britain and abroad and includes the nineteen books (published by The Hogarth Press except where otherwise stated) listed below.

Poetry: *The Storm* (The Orkney Press, 1954), *Loaves and Fishes* (1959), *The Year of the Whale* (1965), *Fishermen with Ploughs* (1971), *Poems New and Selected* (1971), *Winterfold* (1976), *Selected Poems* (1977)

Short stories: *A Calendar of Love* (1967), *A Time to Keep* (1969), *Hawkfall* (1974), *The Sun's Net* (1976)

Short stories for children: *The Two Fiddlers* (Chatto & Windus, 1974), *Pictures in the Cave* (Chatto & Windus, 1977)

Play: *A Spell for Green Corn* (1970)

Novels: *Greenvoe* (1972), *Magnus* (1973)

Essays: *An Orkney Tapestry* (Gollancz, 1969), *Letters from Hamnavoe* (Gordon Wright, 1975)

Memoir: *Edwin Muir* (The Castlelaw Press, 1975)

NOTES

The notes in this edition are intended to serve the needs of overseas students as well as those of British-born users.

Page

3   *Krishna:* Vishnu, a Hindu diety.
    Orkney: called by the Old Irish historians *Insi Orc* ('the islands of the Orcs'), an *orc* being 'a wild boar' and the Orcs the name of a Pictish tribe. The Old Norse name was *Orkneyjar*, afterwards pronounced 'Orkney' by the Scots.
    Johnsmas: St John's Day, Midsummer's Day.
    Kirkwall: the City and Royal Burgh of Kirkwall is situated on the Mainland island of Orkney.

13 *procurator:* prosecutor.

14 *Lammas:* 1 August, the feast of first fruits.

15 *peatstock:* peatstack.

19 *dempster:* or doomster, formerly a Scottish court officer who used to make a formal proclamation of sentence upon the prisoner.

22 *private information:* in 1606 King James VI restored for the second time episcopal rule, and therefore bishops, to the Scottish Presbyterian Church. The bishop in Orkney, James Law, appalled by the tyranny of Earl Patrick Stewart and the distress of the poor eventually sent a letter to the king in 1608 advising him of the sad conditions in the islands. In 1609 the earl was arrested and imprisoned in Edinburgh Castle. He might have escaped punishment had he not prevailed on his natural son Robert to raise a rebellion in Orkney. The rebellion was put down and in 1615 Robert was hanged in Edinburgh and his father

beheaded the following year. Thus, unlamented, ended the barbaric Stewart rule in Orkney.

23   *precentor:* leader of the singing of a church congregation or choir.

    Mary: Mary, Queen of Scots (1542–87).

24   *prebend:* prebendary, a resident clergyman receiving a share of the income of a cathedral or collegiate church.

    Scarlet Woman and Anti-Christ and the Whore of Babylon: the expressions favoured by extreme anti-Catholic Protestants to describe the Church of Rome and its Pope derive from Revelation 17:1–5.

29   *Blessed Sacrament:* the Host (a small circular wafer of unleavened bread).

31   *pyx:* small box used to carry the Host to the sick.

    oil: the holy oils applied to the face and hands during the Sacrament of Extreme Unction (the 'Last Sacrament').

    Domine, non sum dignus: Lord, I am not worthy.

    Host: see note to p. 29.

34   *stewed rabbit:* rabbits are believed to have been introduced to Britain by the Normans in the twelfth century. The earliest known reference to rabbits in Orkney was made in 1693, and the rodents are thought to have first reached the islands during the previous century.

35   *compline:* the seventh and last service of the day, completing the canonical hours (set hours for prayer) of the Roman Catholic Church, takes place at 9 p.m.

    matins: morning song, one of the seven canonical hours, sung between midnight and daybreak.

36   *Hrossey:* 'Horse Isle', the name given by the Norsemen to what is now the Mainland island of Orkney.

41   *A Time to Keep:* see Ecclesiastes 3:1–9.

42   *box-bed:* bed with wooden sides and a roof and a door of two sliding or hinged panels.

45   *Hamnavoe:* the old name for Stromness, where he was born, is used consistently by George Mackay Brown in his stories

and poems.

46 *Martinmas:* 11 November, the feast of St Martin, a term-day in Scotland.

Crofters' Act of 1888: the Act of 1886 gave the crofter perpetual tenure and safeguarded him from eviction subject to certain conditions (e.g. his rent must not fall into arrear for one year, he cannot assign his tenancy, he must not become bankrupt).

The Martyrdom of Man: see note to p. 146.

57 *Robert Burns and Tom Paine:* hypocrisy was not a feature of the lives of the Scottish poet (1759–96) or of the English radical and deist (1737–1809).

64 *'The Harray Crab':* Harray is the only landlocked parish in Orkney.

70 *Lofoten:* Norwegian port.

72 *Session Clerk:* in the Church of Scotland, the official responsible for recording the transactions of the kirk-session (church management committee).

74 *devil's advocate: advocatus diaboli*, an advocate at a papal court charged with the duty of proposing objections to a canonisation; the term is also used to describe someone who purposely argues an opposite view in order to secure a fair appraisal.

81 *Durness:* and Lairg (p. 82) in the modern county of Sutherland were, at the time of the Viking raids in the north of Scotland, part of the district of Caithness which was then bounded on the south by Strath Oykel.

Rousay: like Westray, one of the Orkney islands at that time occupied by the Vikings.

84 *Tithonus:* in legend the lover of Eos who asked the god Zeus to make him immortal, but forgot to ask also for perpetual youth for him. As he began to age Eos wearied of looking after him, turned him into a cicada and imprisoned him in a cage. In Tennyson's early poem Tithonus speaks of his 'cruel immortality' and prays for death.

91 *Agonistes:* the Wrestler.

94 *piece of socialism ... 1882:* see note to p. 46.

103 *via crucis:* way of the cross.

104 *'The Orcadian':* published weekly and established in Kirkwall in 1854 by James Urquhart Anderson, the first newspaper to be printed and published in the Orkney islands.

109 *shut-bed:* box-bed (see note to p. 42).

110 *'Forward':* socialist weekly which was first published in Glasgow in 1906 and ceased publication in 1960.

112 *Pentland Firth:* the sea passage separating the Orkney island from the Scottish mainland.

114 *Dunbeath:* the Caithness birthplace of the novelist Neil Miller Gunn (1891–1973) who appears in the story as Niall the poet. Allusions to four of Gunn's novels occur in the text (p. 114): 'the ballad of the silver shoals in the west' refers to *The Silver Darlings* (1941), 'the boy and the fishing boat' to *Grey Coast* (1926), 'the mysterious well of wisdom' to *The Well at the World's End* (1951), and the 'great song about the salmon' to *Highland River* (1937).

116 *woodbines:* popular brand of cigarettes.

118 *cream cookies:* partly split buns with an insertion of cream.
Bu: the name of many farms in Orkney dates back to the days of the Norse earldom when it described a large farm within a grouping of smaller ones.

131 *W.R.I.:* Women's Rural Institute.

134 *John Bunyan:* (1628–88), English author who, for upholding unlawful meetings, was imprisoned for twelve years and released after the Declaration of Indulgence in 1672. He was re-arrested in 1673, when the Declaration was cancelled, and wrote the first part of his *Pilgrim's Progress* during a further six months' imprisonment.
James Maxton: (1885–1946), a Scottish politician, supporter of the Independent Labout Party and M.P. A conscientious objector, he was imprisoned for attempting to induce a

strike of shipyard workers during the First World War.

Gandhi: Mohandas Karamchand Gandhi (1869–1948), Indian leader, was imprisoned by the British for conspiracy from 1922 to 1924; for various acts of civil disobedience he was arrested in 1930, 1931 and 1942, and finally released in 1944. He was assassinated in 1948 by a Hindu fanatic.

136 *Ramsay Macdonald:* James Ramsay MacDonald (1866–1937), Scottish-born politician, who was Prime Minister and Foreign Secretary of the first British Labour government in 1924.

137 *The Yellow Peril:* the supposed threat to the world of the rising populations of China and Japan, an expression first used by the sensationalist Press of the 1890s.

142 *The Scarlet Woman . . . the Whore of Babylon:* see note to p. 24.

146 *Thinker's Library:* the first of what was to become a famous series was published by C.A. Watts & Co. Ltd in 1929. Clothbound and modestly priced, the books enjoyed a wide readership among radicals, free thinkers and others. Robertson's *Short History of Christianity* appeared as No. 24 in 1931, Reade's *The Martyrdom of Man* as No. 25 in 1932, and Ingersoll's *The Liberty of Man, and Other Essays* as No. 86 in 1941.

Robertson: John MacKinnon Robertson (1856–1933), Scottish writer and politician, was at one time (1891–93) editor of '*National Reformer*', a leading organ of radical free thinkers.

Ingersoll: Robert Green Ingersoll (1833–99), American lawyer, soldier, lecturer and agnostic.

Reade: William Winwood Reade (1838–75), novelist and traveller. *The Martyrdom of Man* (1872), which contained his criticism of religious beliefs, went into many editions.

147 *consummatum est:* it is finished.

149 *transfigured Bread:* the Host – see note to p. 29.

150 *Festival:* the first of the Edinburgh International Festivals was held in 1947.

GLOSSARY

Because there are variations in the meaning and spelling of many Scottish words, some of the explanations given here are appropriate only to the context in which the words are used.

auld old
back backwards
bairn child
bannock home-made flat cake, usually made of oatmeal
bide stay
biding staying
bodies persons
body person
brae hill-slope
brose oatmeal mixed with boiling water or milk and seasoned with butter and salt
bruck rubbish
byre cowhouse
cairn heap of stones used as a landmark, or to mark a grave
clegs gadflies, horse-flies
croft small piece of arable land, usually with a dwelling; a small farm
crofter one who works a croft
cuithe coal-fish between one

and three years old
de'ils devils
dished served
dominie schoolmaster
dour obstinate
dram glass of whisky
dwined dwindled, wasted
fair pretty good
fankle entanglement
forby besides
fore forwards
freshet stream
gang going
girdle griddle
glebe farmland attached to a rural church
glim feeble light
gonner one dead or beyond hope of recovery
goodwife wife
grieve farm manager
hasna has not
howffs public houses, taverns
ken know
kirk church

Glossary

kirkyard churchyard
kirn churn
kye cattle
laird landed proprietor
mam mother
manse parish minister's house
midden dunghill, refuse-heap
muirburn annual burning of moorland
oatcakes thin dry cakes made with oatmeal
on-carry carry-on
owre over
peats blocks dug from bogs for use as fuel
peatstack stack of drying or stored peats
peedie little

puir poor
quernstone stone handmill
reek smoke, fug
ruckle pile, loose heap
scunner dislike, loathing
sillock coal-fish in its first year
sough sigh
stickit stuck, unsuccessful
tattie potato
thee you; your (p. 67)
theeself yourself
thu you
tinker gypsy
trow troll, goblin
wee little
while time; *this while back* some time, recently
whitemaa herring-gull